I0531619

Storylandia

The Wapshott Journal of Fiction

Issue 41

The Wapshott Press

Storylandia, Issue 41, The Wapshott Journal of Fiction, ISSN 1947-5349, ISBN 978-1-942007-41-8 is published at intervals by the Wapshott Press, now a 501(c)(3) nonprofit, PO Box 31513, Los Angeles, California, 90031-0513, telephone 323-201-7147. All correspondence can be sent to The Wapshott Press, PO Box 31513, LA CA 90031-0513. Visit our website at www.WapshottPress.org to learn more. This work is copyright © 2022 by Storylandia. The Wapshott Journal of Fiction, Los Angeles, California. Copyright © 2000-2022 by the authors and are reprinted here with the copyright owner's permission.

Storylandia is always seeking quality original short stories, novelettes, and novellas. Please have a look at our submission guidelines at www.Storylandia.WapshottPress.org or email the editor at editor@wapshottpress.org

Donations happily accepted at www.donate.wapshottpress.org

Cover photograph "Windshield" from www.pixabay.com/photos/road-travel-car-windshield-trip-4510033

Storylandia

The Wapshott Journal of Fiction

Founded in 2009

Issue 41, Spring 2022

Edited by Ginger Mayerson

Contents

Stranded Motorist
by
Jason Feingold
1

Stranded Motorist
by
Jason Feingold

Stranded Motorist

Cheyenne, Wyoming is a nasty, dusty, khaki little burg, at least, what I see of it is. I don't really care. I'm not staying. All I need to do is find the right building, do what I have to do, and get back on the road.

A squat cinderblock building proclaims itself a United States Post Office, and the zip code matches what I wrote down last month. I park in the small lot and try to steel myself for what I have to do next. I put it off. I sit in the car until I feel like someone is going see something and say something. I finally force myself to get out and go inside.

I wait in line for the next available clerk. It's not a long wait. Soon I'm confronted by the unavoidable need to interact with another human being.

"May I help you?" the clerk asks. She is an attractive woman with large brown eyes and long chestnut-brown hair that cascades down her shoulders. Her beauty just makes things harder.

"I should..." I begin, but I choke on the words. I haven't used my voice in a couple of days. Our eyes are locked. We're having a moment. I clear my throat. I want this moment to end.

"I should have an envelope in general delivery," I tell her. "My name is Kenneth White."

"Do you have some ID?" she asks.

I take out my driver's license and hand it to

her. She examines it.

"You're from North Carolina." It isn't a question.

"Yes," I say. It's true, insofar as I'm from anywhere.

"You're a long way from home," she comments.

Home? What is home? I want to say, but I say nothing. She wouldn't understand.

"Let me check," she finally says. She disappears into the back with my license. It's taking her a long time to look. I begin to wonder if I got the right place. I wonder if I look like somebody on the FBI Most Wanted list. Is she calling the police? Finally, to my relief, she returns with the familiar large manila envelope. She hands it to me along with my driver's license.

"Here you go," she says.

"Thanks," I tell her as I begin to walk away.

"No one uses general delivery anymore," she comments before I can make my escape. The moment continues.

"I'm traveling," I tell her.

"Really? Where?"

"Wherever the road takes me."

"Must be nice," she comments.

"It is," I lie. It's a whopper of a lie, but I'll say anything I think she wants to hear to get her to stop talking to me.

"Well, thanks again," I tell her. I make my escape to the lobby. The moment is finally over.

Once I'm out of sight of the postal clerk, I walk over to one of the tables and open the envelope. I turn it upside down and give it a shake. The usual checks spill out. I carefully study each one and sign it. One is for my Visa card, two are for my Master Cards, one is for the upkeep of my house in Charlotte, one is for my car insurance, another for health insurance, one for my accountant, and the last one is, of course, to pay the lawyer who prepared this packet for me at three hundred dollars an hour.

On two prepared forms, I write the date, city, and zip code for when and where I want the next packet sent. Olympia, Washington, 98501. It will be waiting for me when I get there in a month. I fold one copy of the form into eighths and put it in my wallet in case I forget. I stuff the rest of the papers into the self-addressed stamped envelope, seal it, and drop it in the outgoing mail slot in the wall. Another month has come and gone. I've survived.

When I go back out to my car, I notice that the tires look bald. Great. Another stop.

I'm back on the road, finally, following the route I mapped out at a gas station somewhere this morning. I'm heading roughly west and roughly north, and I intend to keep zig-zagging slightly northwest and northeast in long lines until I'm near the Canadian border. I don't dare cross over, though. I'll head in some other direction instead.

I pretend I'm off the grid. I pretend I'm free. I'm not. I have a house, a driver's license, credit cards, and lots and lots of money invested in lots and lots of places. I may constantly be moving around, but I'm on the radar, visible to anyone who cares to look.

No one looks.

I don't know how to live any other way. I'm not Bob Dylan. I don't know how to drop off the map. I'm never nowhere. I'm always somewhere, near one town or another.

~~~

I know in my heart that I am beneath contempt. My guilt is for avoiding life. My penance is driving through this limbo. For all that, I have committed no crime. My car is registered, my license valid, my taxes paid...yet I cannot shake the feeling that they are only half a mile back, closing fast, bringing the worst that can happen with them.

When cars follow me too closely or for too long I ease up on the throttle, ever so slightly until they pass me and slowly drift away. I always drive just above the speed limit, never enough to attract attention, never too close to the number of the law.

Behind tinted glass, I am translucent, bordering on invisible.

Patrol cars are the worst. I can't dismiss them as paranoia. Every time I see one, I try not to look guilty or suspicious, but I know I look like both. I keep my eyes straight ahead, risking a furtive glance every few seconds at it in the mirrors. I don't play with the radio, except to turn it off if it is on. I don't rustle the maps. I don't play with the GPS. I have no radar detector. That would be provocative.

I don't even steer around the bumps on the road for fear of being pulled over for swerving.

Some days, from far away, every luggage rack looks like a police car's light bar. Those are the worst days.

Sometimes I pretend my car can fly. I can almost feel it come off the pavement and gently rise. I go higher and higher until I come to the edge of space. I look down on an Earth where humanity is too small to see.

I like to think about what it would be like to be a Grizzly Adams in the woods and forests through which

I drive. How long and how wide must a meridian strip be to support a human life? I want to have no problems except those at the base of existence: food, clothing, and shelter. I want to be alone, with only my knife and my hatchet, my flint and steel, my thoughts only of survival. Of course, I would die. But who cares? I could simply undo my seat belt, jerk the wheel right or left, and this endless road trip would finally be over.

I am a nation of one between the lane markers of the highway, from my front bumper to my rear spoiler. This metal box is my domain. It is not much, my mobile country, but while it moves, it is invulnerable, never in one place at any given time. If only I could drive forever, immune to sleep and hunger, urination and defecation, filth and entropy, then I could be safe.

John Lennon is playing on the radio. The air conditioner is blasting. The sky is gray. It feels like February, even though it's not.

If John had known what was coming, would have done things any differently? Would he have fled, like me? I like to think he wouldn't have changed his course, that he would have shrugged off any prophetic warnings with a few sarcastic quips, but that would just make him another pointless, useless martyr. I don't think he would have liked that. I know I wouldn't.

We all live under the gun. We just don't appreciate it until the hammer starts to fall. Do we wise up then? No. We go on to delusions of grandeur. We think that somehow, we might be better off, or even worse, that the world might be better off if we were to leave something behind. Most of us don't. The ones who do have been doing it all along.

It must be nice to have that consolation.
Or maybe it doesn't matter.

I must have passed twenty-five churches in the last
hour. It would be so easy to stop at one and declare
my desire for the embrace of a kind and loving God.
The Christians would welcome me. They would shout
words of praise, lay their hands upon me, declare
"Hallelujah!" and taunt the devil with righteous pride
in victory.

But I don't believe. I don't *believe*.

Still, I want to stop moving. I want to belong.
I want all thought to stop, to be in static harmony
with a motionless universe. Nirvana. Heaven. I want
to sluff off each layer of my existence as a dog loses
its winter coat. I want to be blown by the wind until
there is nothing left but air and not even that.

How easy life must be if only one has faith.

Question: How did this happen? How did this come
to be my life? How can I continue to live, or pretend
to live, this way?

Answer: It happened gradually. Then suddenly.

The gradual part took years. The sudden part
happened the night I tried to go home five years ago.
I wasn't tired, and there was no reason I shouldn't
go. I packed a bag and got into my car and drove.
It took many hours. Savoring the expectations of
my homecoming, I stopped for gas, or to use the
bathroom, or to drink a cup of coffee. I remember
how the stillness of the summer night energized me,
broken as it was by the buzz of cicadas and the whirr
of downshifting semis. The aroma of diesel exhaust
and coffee in the right combination will always bring
me back to that first leg of my journey.

When I reached the place where I was born, I drove from place to place all day looking for something familiar, something that spoke of home. I couldn't find it. I tried so hard to run into somebody, anybody I had once known, but there was no familiar face anywhere.

All I found were the bones of my once-flesh life. Here was the house in which I lived, and there was the one next to it. The occupants were strangers. There was the school in which I had learned or failed to learn, but it did not matter. All that was left was the facade. There were no teachers to remember me, even if I could remember them. The inside had been remodeled into apartments, or condominiums, or chambers of solitary confinement.

I felt lost.

My mother told me once that when you get lost you should stay still and wait to be found. But I was not lost. The word "lost" implies there's a place I should be. I do not think there is such a place.

Odysseus was lost, trying to find his way home. Aeneas went to hell to get directions. Hansel and Gretel marked the trail to home with breadcrumbs because they knew they would get lost, because they never lost touch with the value of home.

Moses wandered in the desert for forty years only to find a home he could not enter.

There is no home that could contain me now. I have become only movement, a blur that never comes into full resolve. My dream of home is gone. It's a myth, like God and goodness and the *Odyssey* itself.

In my dreams, I still fall in love. In my dreams, I am still consumed with that pit-of-the-stomach yearning for the woman who has no face and no name. It lingers into waking like the memory of a failed love-affair, still opened and exposed and raw. It fades only in counterpoint to the sound of the engine and the hum of the wheels on the road and the comforting monotony of the mile markers planted firmly with mechanical regularity at the side of the road.

I have a key ring. I got it when I bought the car. On the key ring is a single key, the key to my car. Everything I need is contained somewhere within the car.

The car has no name.

In the trunk, there are two laundry baskets. One has clean clothes, and the other gradually fills with dirty clothes. When I'm down to my last pair of clean underwear, I go looking for a laundromat. If I can't find one that doesn't frighten me, I buy more clean clothes and leave the dirty ones behind.

I do not like the feel of clothes that have not been washed, but I like the feel of an impoverished laundromat even less. It is everything that is wrong with the world.

Sunrises are so peaceful. Only those with the best intentions are out and on the road. At least, that's the way it feels. School buses and milkmen. Newspaper delivery trucks. Donna Reed putting on her heels and pearls to make bacon and eggs for her family.

America the way it's supposed to be.

I especially like rest stops during sunrise. All the evildoers have long since passed out, and there's no one but long-haul truckers and young families on their way to something better. Some are already beaten down. Some still have a semblance of hope in their eyes. Either way, it's exhilarating.

In the morning, I feel safest. If I am ever gently

lulled towards sleep, it is in those minutes that I grow somnolent and seek the refuge of a moderately-priced motel. They are quiet in the mornings, too, except for the sounds of the maids cleaning and people shuffling down the halls, struggling with their luggage.

Motel rooms have a certain smell. In some rooms it's stronger, in some it's in the background, but it's always there. It's a smell that tells you that you are not at home. It gets in your hair, permeates your clothes, and if you stay in enough motel rooms, it is always with you, reminding you of what's not there.

I used to love that smell.

When I check in, I'm tired, tired to the point of staggering. It is the only way I will sleep. Clerks look at me funny or look like they don't care. It doesn't matter to me either, as long as they give me the room.

In the room I retreat into sleep, my only refuge from the world I've made. When I'm lucky, my sleep is a long black place from which I take no memories. Most of the time, though, I dream of things I dare not dwell on for fear they will paralyze me with the inertia of karma and regret. I wake up and turn on the television, and eventually, the feelings go away.

Sometimes I think about sex. I don't think of it as much as I used to, and I think even less about it as time goes on and the miles rack up. It's like thinking about one's youth. At times, one can be wistful, but by the same token, one realizes that it can't be returned to. It is gone forever, and, like youth, that isn't necessarily a bad thing.

I used to yearn for it, but it turns out that sex isn't what I wanted after all. I was just lonely.

I'm not sure how much longer I can keep this up.

Somewhere, sometime, something has got to give. It could be any time now. Where will I be when I stop?

I suppose I am a sociopath. I walked away from everything that was normal, wholesome, and good: wife, children, home, and all of the trappings of the Dream American. I ran that life into the ground like a spare car, and when I left, I felt nothing. They were better off without me.

At least there is the money.
The money was an unexpected accident of inheritance. I did not earn it. I did not expect it. It fell into my lap and made me its slave. I husband it. I shepherd it. I pay people to guard it. I spend only what is necessary to live, and that includes staying in motion. The only luxury is my car, but it is not luxurious enough to attract undue attention. It's not a Cadillac, but rather a few rungs down from the top.

Even though most of my time is spent behind the wheel, I am thin for the first time in my life. I've had to stop and buy clothes as the pounds melt off me. At least the less I eat, the less I have to use the bathroom. Perhaps like Siddhartha, I will starve myself into enlightenment while sitting in the shadow cast by the roof of my Ford 500.

It was inevitable that I would get pulled over sooner or later. As I wait for the state trooper to come to the window, I begin to sweat big fat drops of guilt-sweat I try to wipe away with my hand. What I can see of myself in the rear-view mirror isn't good. I'm unkempt and bushy-bearded, and my hair is too long.
Finally, the cop approaches, and I roll down the

window after fumbling the key to the access setting.

"Did you know your left brake light is out?" he asks. My car has betrayed me. My nation of one is in rebellion. There is a crack in my cocoon.

"No. I'm sorry," I say, feeling the trembling in my voice and unable to hide it.

"Let me see your license and registration."

I give him both. He goes back to his car. It takes an agonizing five minutes for him to come back. Am I wanted? I have a lawyer, but he's thousands of miles away, back where I started from. I have been cultivating loneliness, but I've never felt so alone as I do with this policeman. He is the sentinel of all things normal. I am an aberration trying to slide away through the cracks in the pavement.

The trooper comes back with a clipboard. I can see my license and registration on it. The address on both documents is almost fictitious. It's the address of my lawyer's office.

"You're a long way from home," he observes. "Where are you headed?"

"Seattle," I say, but I take too long to answer. Not only is there now contact between us, but there is also suspicion.

"What's in Seattle?"

"Family. Cousins."

"You're driving all the way from North Carolina to Seattle?" he asks, flicking my driver's license with his finger.

"I'm afraid of flying."

I can see in his face he thinks my lies are floating on the top of a greater truth. A nefarious truth. An underhanded truth.

"Take the key out of the ignition. Step out of the car," he says. "Walk around to the back and put your hands on the trunk."

"Why?" I ask.

"Because I said so," he replies. I am the child. He is the stern father, a patriarch of the highway. I do what he says.

"Do you have anything in your pockets that's going to stick me?" he asks.

"No."

He pats me down. He retrieves my wallet from my pants. After going through it, he places it on the roof of the car.

"Now open the trunk."

I don't want to, but I'm too afraid to say no. He pokes around in my clean and dirty laundry baskets and rummages through my toilet kit. He takes everything out of the trunk and lifts up the carpeting to inspect the spare tire well.

"No suitcases," he observes, poking through my laundry baskets. I say nothing. No matter what I say, he will reach the conclusions he is going to reach with or without my help.

He orders me to stand on the shoulder while he rummages through my car with a flashlight. I have two thousand dollars rolled up and jammed underneath the seat. It's my emergency money. I hope he doesn't find the roll of cash, but of course, he does.

"What's this?" he asks, holding the money.

"My emergency money," I tell him.

"Why did you hide it?"

"So no one would find it."

He doesn't put the cash on the roof of the car with my wallet. He puts it in his pocket. I have a feeling it's going to stay there.

"There's no law against carrying money," I say, frightened but growing furious.

"How do I know it isn't drug money?" the officer asks.

"I don't know. How about the fact that I don't have any drugs?"

"Are you getting smart with me?"

"No. I just want my money back."

"Ever heard of asset forfeiture?"

"No."

"If I suspect that this money is being used for illegal purposes, I can seize it."

"Without a trial?"

"Without a trial. And you, my friend, are suspicious."

"You're going to steal my money," I accuse.

"Seize it," he corrects me.

"Can I get a receipt?" I ask.

"No."

He tosses my license and registration on the roof of the car next to my wallet, gets in his car, and drives away. I have no name and no car number to identify him. I'm not even sure what state I'm in. The money is definitely gone, as gone as it would have been if I had burned it.

My worse paranoid fantasy has just played itself out, and I have survived it, less my little nest egg. The money is easily replaced, but I am as angry for not standing up for myself as I am with the crooked cop. As I put my things back in the trunk, I begin to shake all over.

I still have my credit cards and about five hundred dollars the cop neglected to steal from my wallet along with all the rest. The first thing I plan to do is to find a bank and cash advance myself another two grand of just-in-case money. I don't feel as armored as I did when I had it, and my armor was already thin.

~ ~ ~

"What do you mean, declined?" I ask incredulously. I have no idea what the limit is on the credit card, but I bought my current car with it, so it must be pretty high. Two thousand dollars shouldn't be a problem.

"That's all I know," says the teller.

"There must be some glitch in the system. Try this one instead." I snap another plastic card on the counter. It too is declined. Ditto with the third and fourth.

"Why is this happening?" I ask the teller.

"I don't know," she says. "You should probably call them."

I go back to my car shaking, my legs unsteady beneath me. There's no way the money could have run out. Something is very wrong.

I take the prepaid cell phone I bought for emergencies out of the glove box. Of course, the battery is dead, and it takes me a while to figure out how to plug it in. I call each of the credit card companies, and each one tells me that I'm delinquent on my payments and the card has been shut off. I am scared and furious, and I have one more call to make.

I know the number of the law firm I've entrusted with my financial being by heart, and I punch in the numbers.

"Olvido, Patton, and Hart," says a pretty voice on the other end. "How may I direct your call?"

"I need to talk with Mr. Patton," I say. "My name is Ken White. I need to talk to him now."

"I'm sorry, sir," says the pretty voice. "Attorney Patton died in a car crash two months ago."

"Who took over his cases?" I ask.

"We're still sorting that out," she says.

"Look, Mr. Patton was supposed to be paying

my credit card bills, and he hasn't. All of my cards were declined. I'm the middle of nowhere. There has to be someone who can take care of that for me. His secretary, maybe?"

"She was also killed in the crash," says the pretty voice, more sad than attractive now.

"I'm sorry to hear that," I say, even though I'm not sorry for anyone but myself. "How long do you think it's going to take to get this straightened out?"

"I don't know," she says.

"Okay. Who does know?"

"I can transfer you to Attorney Olvido," she says.

"Yes. Do that."

I don't get Olvido, but I do get his voicemail. It's hard to leave a message asking him to call me back when I don't know the number of the phone I'm using, but I outline my problem and tell him to expect me in a couple of days, and that I hope things will be straightened out before I get there.

I am distraught. I don't know where I am, and I only have five hundred dollars to get back to Charlotte where the lawyers' office is. I hope it will be enough. The Ford 500 isn't the best mileage vehicle I've ever owned.

I put my destination into the GPS. I'm somewhere in Washington State. What I hoped was a two-thousand-mile trip is closer to three thousand. I'll have to stick to the interstates. The GPS estimates the driving time at forty-two hours. I think I can do it in six days if I drive twelve hours a day, six days of insecurity, hour after hour of fearing what might go wrong. And I only have five hundred dollars. I have to pay for gas, food, and a place to flop every now and then.

For the first time in five years, time is finite.

It feels strange to me. I never imagined it could come to this. I thought I had enough safeguards to prevent this from happening.

Having a destination upsets me. What upsets me more is that I have to delay getting started on the trip because I have to replace the brake light. Being on a schedule ratchets that discomfort up like a car jack.

    I find an auto parts store and buy a bulb. I try to change it myself in the parking lot, but I don't have the necessary tools, so I have to go back into the store and buy those too. I wonder if it would have been cheaper to just find a garage to do it for me.

    After checking all the lights on the car, I make my way to I-90. I ease the car up to seven miles an hour over the speed limit, taking a chance of getting pulled over again. For the first time in five years, I have a purpose. There is meaning behind each mile I put behind me. I have direction. I have danger. I'm in trouble.

    I don't know what I'll do if I don't get to Charlotte before the money runs out. There is no one to help me. I wanted to be alone. That was the whole point. Now the idea scares the shit out of me. It is amazing how desires can turn on the head of a pin.

    As I make my way east, I drive until the fuel light is shining brightly on my dashboard. I want to squeeze every mile per gallon out of the Ford as I can. Each fill-up costs around forty dollars, and I can squeeze thirty miles per gallon out of the tank. Between gas and food, I should make it to my destination with two hundred dollars to spare if I sleep in the car. It seems like my existence is hanging by a very narrow thread.

    I'll make it, though. I will begin my endless trip anew. Next time I'll pay more attention to who is doing what with my money. I'll hire two lawyers. This can never happen again.

I feel like I'm playing a game of hide and seek, trying to stay safely tucked away until someone calls "Allie-allie-in free!" But hiding isn't an option for me. I have to outrun "it." I have to be evasive, anonymous, invisible, and I can be none of those things when I have to be in a particular place by a particular time.

The first day of driving brings me to the confluence of I-90 and I-15. There are lots of hotels, but I can't afford to stay in any of them. I find a truck stop and reluctantly take a shower and wash my dirty clothes, resenting every dollar I have to spend. Clean for the first time in two days, I eat my fill at the buffet. I eat until I'm stuffed. Every dollar has to pull its weight. I shouldn't have to eat for at least another day, maybe two.

I put my car in the most remote place on the truck stop lot I can find. I recline the seat and sleep. It is a shallow, fitful thing at first. The need to get to Charlotte keeps worrying me and waking me, but I'm in no shape to drive, so I force myself to rest and eventually fall into a deeper, more restful sleep.

I am awakened by banging on the window. I open my eyes. The faint light in the sky tells me that it's early in the morning. I pull my seat into an upright position and look for the source of the noise. She is framed by the passenger door's window. She's no Carol Brady. She looks like a truck stop hooker. I've seen them in action, but I've never been approached by one. I have no interest in a cheap, tawdry hookup. I shake my head no, hoping she'll go away. I want no intimacy; especially not the kind that's sold by the minute.

She persists.

"Let me in," she shouts through the closed window. I turn the car key to access and roll the window down ever so slightly.

"I'm not interested," I tell her.

"Please, mister. I just need a ride. Just to the next truck stop. Please." For the first time, I notice how nervous she looks, how she keeps looking around as if death is lingering in every direction.

I should roll the window up and be on my way, but I don't. For some reason, I can't.

"I've got money," she says. "I'll pay you. Just get me out of here."

Before I know it, the locks have snapped open. She gets in the car, stinking of cheap perfume. Her clothes are too short and too tight, and she looks permanently tired.

"Go!" she orders. "He's coming."

I turn to look at what she's looking at. I see a man exit a red truck with a trailer that reads "Benson Hauling" attached. He's carrying a tire iron. What have I gotten myself into? He can't possibly mean her any good with a blunt steel instrument in his hand, and since I let her into my car, he can't possibly mean me any good either.

I start the engine and pop it into drive. As I speed away, I hear the sound of metal on metal. He's thrown the tire iron at my car. This strengthens my resolve to speed toward the truck stop's exit and onto the I-90 entrance ramp. It's not until we're on the highway that I realize my seatbelt isn't on. I fasten it and tell the hooker to fasten hers. I'll never get the cheap perfume smell out of the car. Once my business in Charlotte is settled, I'll have to buy a new one.

It takes a while, but my adrenaline finally

dissipates. Her's must have decayed at the same rate.

"I'm Jade," she says.

"I'm John," I stammer, lying. I don't know how long it's been since I had to introduce myself. "A. John."

"Aren't you clever."

I didn't think she'd get it. I'm ashamed for having said it.

"What did that guy want? The one who banged up my car?"

"He wanted me to do something that I don't do. Then he asked for a refund, which is something I also don't do. I'm sorry about your car."

"That's okay," I sighed. "It's probably easier to get fixed than what he was going to do to you with that tire iron."

"Yeah."

"So where is this truck stop you want me to take you to?"

"It's about two hundred miles away. Just keep driving east."

"How do you know he won't just look for you there?"

"They usually don't stop so soon, these long-haul truckers," she said. "They have schedules they have to keep. Anyway, I'll take my chances."

I want to be indifferent about it, but I can't. I care. She's like me, on the run with no real destination in mind. I live off money that I didn't earn. She lives on money she shouldn't earn, at least not that way. We are creatures that exist on the same spectrum, somewhere between light and darkness, in the grey areas of the world.

Jade sleeps in the passenger seat. I have no doubt that she had a busy night. I cannot really imagine what her life is like, and I'm pretty sure I don't want to know. How many enemies has she made? What if the man with the tire iron finds us?

I feel even more vulnerable with the hooker riding beside me. Now I must fear every truck I pass or passes me. I should have simply driven away and left her to her fate. I have enough problems of my own. There was no need to take on the woman's problems as well. But I'm lying to myself. I could no sooner turn her away as I could watch a baby try to crawl across a highway. All that time on the road, all that time in the metaphorical desert, and it has not hardened me one iota.

"Where are we?" Jade asked wearily, stretching her limbs and straining her tight clothes to the breaking point.

"Somewhere near Idaho," I reply.

"You missed the truck stop," she said, her voice dripping a mixture of anger and fear.

"I know," I said. "I didn't like the idea of leaving you stranded."

"What do you want from me? Money? Sex?"

"No. I just want to take you someplace safe."

She laughed.

"Home?" she asked.

"Sure," I replied. "Home."

"Well, I don't have one."

"What?"

"I go from truck stop to truck stop fucking and sucking guys off until I have enough for a room and a meal. When the money runs out, I get a ride to the next truck stop and do it all over again."

I am shocked. I am speechless. Five years on the road and I had no idea this underbelly existed.

"I could set you up someplace," I said. "I have money."

"Sure," she said. It sounds like she's heard the line before.

"Seriously. I just need to get to Charlotte and straighten a few things out. You're welcome to come with me."

What the hell am I saying to her? Why am I saying it? I should leave her at a truck stop or a rest area as soon as I can.

"I need a place to change," she says, not deciding one way or the other. I get off at the next exit and pull up to a gas station. She goes into the ladies' room with the big bag she's been carrying. While she's in there, I think about leaving. It would be so easy. All I have to do is start the car and take off up the entrance ramp and never see her again. But I don't. She's a human stray, and I can't just leave her there.

When she comes out of the bathroom, she's dressed in jeans, a flannel shirt, and running shoes. Her makeup is nearly rubbed away. Even the scent of cheap perfume is muted. She looks non-hooker-y. She looks normal. She gets back into the car.

"You're still here," she remarks.

"I thought about leaving," I admit.

"Why didn't you?"

"It would be wrong."

"You don't owe me anything. I can just catch a ride with a truck driver. I've done it often enough."

"You owe me," I say.

She sighs. "How do you want it?"

"Not what you're thinking."

"I've seen *Pretty Woman*," she says. "Is that what you're after? The whore with a heart of gold? Because I ain't got one. I'm just a lot lizard. That's all."

"And I'm just a man trying to get home."
"Where's that? Charlotte?"
"No, not Charlotte. I don't know where. But I'll know it when I see it."

But I don't see it. I never do. Home is never visible from the highway. It's all just motels and fast food restaurants and gas stations and tourist traps of the same thirty-one flavors and combinations.

Jade and I have nothing to say to each other. I am the bird, and she is the broken wing. Together we complete nothing. She stares out the window, and I stare at the road. The enormity of nowhere stretches out in front of us. It constantly swallows us and spits us up again whole. It is worse than being alone, this being alone with somebody else. There is a rift within the car that cannot be crossed, no matter if she is within my arm's reach.

I want to feel nothing for her, but I do. I feel responsible for her even though she seems equipped to fight her own battles. I don't want to be responsible for her. I don't want to be responsible for anybody, hence these five years on the road, far from the woman who was my wife, far from the children who were my children. Sometimes I wonder what's become of them, and when that happens, I'll do just about anything to push those thoughts from my head again.

We stop for food and fuel. Jade insists on paying for half the gas and her lunch at Denny's. Her money is a crumpled ball of fives and tens and twenties that she does not count. I suppose that when the crumpled ball is gone, she'll have me find a truck stop for her and turn more tricks, leaving me to continue on my not-so-merry way. It is not an enviable future, but mine is as bad as hers. Once I get my money sorted out, I'll be back on the road, fleeing from myself at five miles an hour over the speed limit, around and around with no end in sight except the inevitability of stopping someday and never starting again.

When we go back to the car, I consider not unlocking the passenger door for her and speeding away again. I can't. There is some sort of unspoken pact between she and me, and I pop the lock open, and we are on our way again, my face to the road and hers toward the window.

The silence becomes increasingly intolerable. One of us must break it, and it is like a game of chicken to see who will do it first.

I forgot to call Olvido again. Jade has got me completely turned around. She's broken my carefully constructed world. I pull off and call Olvido's office again.

Jade listens to the conversation with great interest. When I glance over at her, her face is speculative and uncertain, like a puppy seeing snow for the first time. I bet she's wondering whether or not I really do have money.

They still don't know what's going on with my business. To make matters worse, they can't schedule another call with Olvido until Friday. It's Tuesday—at least, that's what they tell me. It looks like I will have to go all the way to Charlotte to get this shit fixed.

"It looks like it's going to storm," I say, my eyes on a towering cumulonimbus cloud above the road in front of us.

"I like storms," she says.

I would have thought she hates storms because she might get soaking wet on the lots.

"Really?"

"They wash away the filth," she says. "I like the way they make things smell. Fresh."

Of course, she would say that.

"They're hard to drive through," I comment.

"Never been my problem," she says curtly. Our conversation must be over.

We drive into the storm. Jade must be happy because it is a very strong one. A lot of filth must be washing away. Many cars are pulled off onto the shoulder, waiting it out. I keep moving at the speed of the car in front of me, my windshield wipers slapping away the water as fast as they can. Lightning strikes in a field not too far from the highway. We see a tree totally engulfed in flames despite the downpour that comes in sheets instead of drops.

It does not take long for us to come out the other side. I slow the wipers and then stop them completely. I turn the headlights off so only the daytime running lights are on. I speed up to seven miles an hour over the speed limit, and the wind whips the car dry. In half an hour it is like the storm never happened. Jade rests her head against the window and closes her eyes. Her resting face is etched in doubt and pessimism and sarcasm.

I am sliding in and out of sleep.

"Jade," I say softly. She does not hear me. "Jade," I say again, a little louder.

"What?" she answers, acerbic.

"Do you have a driver's license?"

"No."

"Then we have to stop."

"Why?"

"I'm falling asleep."

"There's a rest stop about fifteen minutes from here. Can you make it that far?"

"I guess. Just keep an eye on me."

Having an immediate destination revives me, and I stop nodding off. Jade watches me closely anyway. She wants to live. When we get there, I guide the car into a space that is not too close and not too far from the building that houses the bathrooms and the vending machines. I set my watch for three hours and recline my seat.

"What am I supposed to do?" she asks.

"Whatever you want," I reply.

"I'm awake now," she complains.

Sleeps takes me before I can reply. I don't want to say anything anyway.

My watch dutifully rings. My three hours are up. I put my seat back upright and stretch. I want to go back to sleep but staying more than a few hours in a rest stop invites a conversation with state troopers, one I'd rather not have. Jade is nowhere to be seen. I imagine she is on the truck side of the rest stop plying her trade. I made no arrangements with her, and she owes me nothing, not even a goodbye.

I get out of my car and lock the door. In the bathroom, I relieve myself and wash my face. I buy a watery cup of coffee from a vending machine and drink it while I look at the "You Are Here" map framed and mounted on the wall. I have so far to go and scant resources to get me there.

When I was in college in the 90's, I would drive the three and a half hours between my parents' house and school in a 1981 VW Rabbit, sometimes with no more than five dollars in my wallet, and I wasn't afraid. Now I have a hundred times that and

I'm scared shitless of everything that can go wrong. God damn that lawyer for leaving me hanging like this, and God damn the firm for not taking up the slack.

I leave the building. I see Jade sitting on the hood smoking a cigarette and waiting for me. It's three in the morning or something like that, and there's a chill in the air. The cicadas are buzzing summertime, and I find it energizing—or maybe it's just the coffee leaking caffeine into my bloodstream. As I get closer, I see that she's wearing her slutty outfit again. There is no need to ask her what she was doing while I was sleeping.

"Sticking around?" I ask her as I get close to the car.

"Might as well," she says. "It's not like I have any place to go. Mind if I change first?"

"Be my guest."

She changes her clothes right there in the parking lot on the far side of the car. I turn away, and she laughs at me.

"You're shy," she says.

"I just want to keep our relationship strictly amateur," I reply.

Three hours of sleep isn't much, but it buys me more driving time. Five years of driving has brought me only to this, to buying time by the hour, from the infinite to the finite. Running to instead of running away.

The sun rises, and we drive right into it. It's too low on the horizon, so I hold my hand up to block its rays as I drive. Jade is asleep again. The sunlight paints her face in stark relief. Some part of me expects her to burst into flames in the sun's beam. She seems to me like a creature of the night. I don't want to rouse her, but the car needs gas, and I need more coffee and something to eat. I choose an exit that boasts both food and fuel. She wakes up as I bring the car to a stop at the bottom of the ramp.

"Where are we?" she asks.

"Idaho, I think."

"Why are we stopping?"

"Food and gas."

"What food?"

"McDonald's."

"I don't want that crap."

"I'm sorry."

"Okay. What do you want?"

"Just stay on this road and drive. Something will pop up."

I find the gas station with the lowest price and gas up. I don't know if I'll need the extra few cents it saves me, but I'd rather have it and not need it. Jade sits in the car and silently hands me money for half the tank when I get back into the car. We start driving down the road as she directed.

The place is a hole-in-the-wall, but Jade insists on stopping here. We're ten miles from I-15. I don't like it. It isn't safe. But she's paying for half of the gas, and it's not really my place to say no anyway. I have no authority over her, and if I tried to exert some, I'm sure she would simply ditch me.

She orders a "monster cheeseburger," and I have what she's having.

"I thought you didn't want hamburgers," I say.

"No, I don't want McDonald's," she rejoins. "This will be different. Trust me."

"Have you been here before?" I ask.

"No, but I've been to enough places like this."

I think about the idea of trust. I hadn't realized it, but there is a molecule of trust between us. She trusts that I won't kill her and leave her in a ditch. She trusts that I won't rape her or make unwanted sexual advances. She trusts that I won't leave her behind. I trust that she won't steal from me or kill me in my sleep or take my car while I'm in the bathroom.

The monster burger lives up to its name. There must be half a pound of beef in it along with onion rings and a fried egg, of all things. I make numerous attempts to pick the thing up without it falling apart. Finally, I use my knife and fork and cut it into pieces to eat it. Jade is watching, and she laughs at me.

"Let's see you do better," I challenge, slightly miffed.

She nimbly picks up her burger and takes a chunk out of it before setting it down again. A hundred jokes, all in bad taste, run through my mind, but I only use my tongue to taste the chunks of burger as I shovel in fork-full after fork-full.

I'm about halfway through the sandwich when I hear a bevy of screaming motorcycles outside. Instead of passing by, they pull into the restaurant's parking lot and put down their kickstands. They're not amateurs. They have angel wings on the backs of their denim vests and leather jackets.

"Oh, shit," I say out loud. This is why I'd never stop at a place like this on my own. My senses scream danger. I want to get up and drive away, but my black Ford is surrounded by a sea of bikes and dust kicked up from the gravel lot.

"It'll be okay," Jade says. "They're like bumble bees. If you leave them alone, they'll leave you alone. Just like most other people."

I'm not reassured. Every biker scene from every

movie I've ever seen involving bikers is parading through my head, and none of them are pleasant.

"We should go," I say.

"Finish your food," Jade commands.

I can't eat another bite. I'm full of burger as well as fear.

The bikes stop roaring in increments until they're all silent. Bikers begin to filter into the restaurant. I'm relieved to see that there are several women among them, rough-looking as they may be. They're not all rogue males.

We are quickly surrounded by bikers on all sides of our booth. The formerly empty restaurant is now almost full. There are about forty bikers and their women. The two waitresses wade into the deluge, unafraid, taking orders and bringing beverages, including beer. More than a few bikers glance at us with bemused expressions on their faces. 'What are they doing here,' I can see them wonder. We are further from the beaten path of the interstate that most John Q. Publics and their wives and girlfriends go. They are assessing us. I feel like a game animal.

"We should go," I repeat, glancing around. The room smells unpleasantly of dirt and sweat.

She smiles at me. "Don't show fear," she mumbles through the pleasant and relaxed expression she has plastered on her face. "You might insult them."

"What?"

"How do you feel when someone acts afraid of you for no reason?" she asked.

"I wouldn't know. I feel bad, I guess."

"Maybe angry?"

"I don't know."

We stare at each other. She's coolly in control of herself. I'm less so. I try to flash a smile across the table at her, but I can't work one up.

"What do we do?" I ask after a few moments.

"Pay the check, leave a tip, and ask them to move," Jade suggests.

"I thought you said to leave them alone."

"You got a better idea? Do you really want to wait until they leave?"

I don't.

Just as she finishes talking, a waitress conveniently plunks the check down on the table. I examine it and leave a twenty-five percent tip. Jade nods, and we get up and take the check to the register. We take our time, hoping whoever owns the bike behind my car will realize on his own that I'm blocked in and move it of his own volition. No one does. I keep standing by the register, feeling conspicuous.

"Excuse me, sir," Jade says to the nearest biker, surprising me. "Do you know who has us blocked in?"

I get the feeling I got when I saw *Easy Rider,* except we're drivers who are going to be killed by bikers instead of bikers being killed by drivers. The biker takes a look out the window.

"Hey, Stash!" he calls across the room. "Your bike is behind this guy!"

"Fuck the guy!" the man I presume is Stash calls back. He has a fierce blond handlebar battle-mustache, hence his name, I suppose. "I'm eating!"

The room becomes quiet. Everyone is looking, their faces reflecting an almost polite interest in what is going to happen next. I'm kind of curious about that myself. I can't let the challenge go unanswered. I'll lose whatever face I have with Jade and with myself. On the other hand, this guy is big. Kicking the shit out of me would present no challenge to him. I haven't been in a fight in forty years.

"Be reasonable," I say to Stash. "I'd move for you."

"You're goddamn right you would."

"Please. We're on a schedule."

"You can wait until I'm done." He takes a small sip of his beverage as a sample of how long he plans to take.

"Dude, just move," says the biker that Jade asked.

"Fuck that."

I see red. The anger comes upon me, so suddenly it's like someone flipped a switch. I feel powerful. The last time I felt like this was so long ago I can't remember if I ever have. Jade feels it too, and she puts a restraining hand on my shoulder, but I shrug it off. I walk over to Stash's table. He gets up to meet me. We get in each other's faces.

"Move. Your. Piece-of-shit. Bike."

Instead of moving it, he shoves me into the table behind me. I'm ready for it, but it doesn't matter. Glasses tip over and plates clink together. I'm off-balance. In half a second, he's going to be on me, swinging away. I'm going to take a beating. I struggle to regain my balance and meet his charge. Whether or not I can do it becomes immaterial. Three guys interpose themselves between him and me. I'm still furious. I try to push through them to get at Stash, but compared to them I've got all the strength of a six-week-old kitten.

"You need to go," one of them says. He must be the alpha male. "Benjy, push Stash's bike out of the way." Benjy goes outside, but I stay where I am. Stash and I have locked eyes, and neither of us is going to be the first to break contact. Jade comes across the room and stands between us, forcing us to stop the staring contest. She tugs my arm so hard I almost lose my balance again.

"Let's go, big boy," she says. She drags me out the door and to the car. We get in. I drive away, pushing the Ford into the red as we speed away. It's not good for the car, but being dead is worse. Fortunately, I see no motorcycles in the rear-view mirror.

We reach the interstate. We get on. We speed away.

We are safe.

"I didn't think you had that in you," Jade says after a few miles whiz by.

"Me neither."

"Are you a mule?" Jade asks as we cruise down the road.

"A mule?"

"You know. Drugs."

"No," I say. "Do I look like a mule?"

"Not really." Pause. "So what do you do?"

"I drive."

"That's it?"

"That's it."

"What do you do for money?"

"Money's not a problem. Well, it won't be a problem once I get to Charlotte."

"But right now, money is a problem," she says.

"Uh huh."

"You're full of shit," she says. "Money is always a problem. It doesn't matter where you go."

"Is that why you go from truck stop to truck stop? Because it doesn't matter where you go?"

"Don't judge me."

"I'm not. I'm the last person who can judge someone on how they live their life."

We grow silent and watch the road. No matter what, there is always the road.

~~~

We're not driving long before I notice a truck approaching us. I don't give it much thought. It will no doubt pass us.

Except it doesn't, even though the passing lane is clear.

I move over into the left lane to let the asshole go by. He must be one of these jerks who doesn't feel he should have to change lanes because of his right of weight. I've seen enough of them before. But instead of blowing by me on the right, he changes lanes too.

"Okay," I murmur. I move back over to the right lane. So does he.

That's when I notice that the truck's cab is red.

Oh, shit.

First the bikers, now this. It must be Judgment Day. Jade is the fucking angel of death.

I put the pedal down. The car drops into a lower gear and roars until I'm up to ninety on the highway. The tachometer needle is well into the red once again. The truck is still closing, but not as fast as it was before. It's just the two of us on this particular stretch of road. No obstructions. No witnesses. No exits. Fuck.

"What the hell?" Jade asks.

I jerk my thumb over my shoulder.

"Is that him?" she asks, turning to look out of the back window.

"How many guys in red trucks have you pissed off?" I ask.

She's silent.

"What did you do to this guy?"

"It's more what I didn't do," Jade says. In other circumstances, it would have been funny.

The highway rises gradually until we're on a steep hill. I keep up my speed, but the truck begins to lag behind. I coax a few more miles an hour out of my Ford. It's still running in the red. Finally, the truck drops back below the horizon. I take the first exit I see and hide behind a gas station until I'm sure he's passed us.

"How did he find us?" I ask Jade.

"He tagged your car," she says. "That's why he threw the tire iron."

"You could have shared this with me sooner."

"I wasn't sure until now," she said. "I thought he was just angry."

"Well, that's terrific. I don't have the money to get it fixed or get another car or get it painted or something."

"He's passed us now," Jade says. "He's long gone."

"How come you haven't asked me to fuck you?" Jade asks all of a sudden. "Are you gay or something?"

"No," I reply. "I'm not gay."

"So why not? Are you a church person?"

"No."

"Then why?"

"I don't want to fuck anyone. Besides, I don't think I'd enjoy it with a..."

"Hooker?"

"I don't want to call you names."

"It's not a name. It's what I am."

"It's what you do."

"I don't get it."

"Don't confuse who you are with what you do to survive."

She laughs at me with a mirthless, scoffing sound.

"And, besides, it's just a job for you," I say. "That doesn't turn me on."

"I don't believe you. All men are horn dogs," she counters.

"You don't have to believe me if you don't want to."

"I don't."

I shrug.

"If you've been driving for five years, how long since you fucked someone?"

"About eight years."

"Eight years? And you don't want to fuck me?"

"That about sums it up, yeah."

The moment I've been dreading has arrived. I have to stop and sleep in a real bed, take a shower, and all those things most people in America take for granted.

"I need to stop and get a room," I tell Jade. "I need a decent night's sleep, or I'm going to kill us both."

"Okay," she says.

There is a pointed silence.

"What are you going to do?"

"Stay with you. It's not like I have to be somewhere."

Off the highway, there is a Hampton Inn. I'd rather find something cheaper, but I'm in no shape to be picky. I drive up to the office to check in.

"One room or two?" I ask her.

"We can split a room," she says.

"You trust me? How do you know I'm not a psychopath?"

"If you were crazy you'd have done something by now. You wouldn't be the first one to try."

"You're kidding."

"I wish."

"How did you fight him off?"

A can of mace comes out of nowhere and is

stuck in my face. It scares the hell out of me. I guess I've been thinking this whole time that she's somehow helpless because of the pissed-off trucker who was chasing her with the tire iron. It was stupid to think of her as a hooker in distress in every situation.

"I'll get the room," I say, and I do just that. Soon we are installed with our things in a room on the top floor at the end of the hall. I always get a room at the end of the hall to cut my chances in half of having to listen to a couple screwing in the next room.

"I'd like to undress," I tell Jade. "I don't really have any pajamas."

"Go ahead. You probably don't have anything I haven't seen before."

"Could you just wait in the bathroom until I get into bed?"

"Are you kidding?"

"Please."

She does what I ask. I strip down to my boxers and get into bed.

"Is it safe?" she asks sardonically from the bathroom.

"Yes."

She comes out of the bathroom in a t-shirt and panties. The sight of her stirs my libido just a little bit, but I quash that feeling by remembering to myself what I am and what she does. Instead of taking the other bed, she gets into bed with me.

"I don't want to..." I begin.

"I know," she says. "It's okay." She puts a pillow between us.

I flick the light off, and in seconds I am gone.

According to my watch, I have slept for ten hours. I sit up onto the edge of the bed, conscious of the loose skin of my middle-age belly for the first time in ages. Jade is nowhere to be found. Her bag is missing too, so the next thing I do is check my wallet. My money is still there. I'm angry with myself for not trying to conceal it before I went to sleep, but I'm also proud for some reason to find out that Jade isn't a thief.

One of the card keys is missing, and there's a wet towel on the bathroom floor. I take a shower and add another wet towel to the collection. I shave for the first time in a long time. It's slow going, but I manage to scrape the hair off my face before the razor gets as blunt as a baseball bat. I'm in the middle of dressing when I hear the lock click open. Jade comes in with two coffees in a holder, a white paper bag held between her teeth, and the bag she keeps all her shit in. She sets the mess on the table.

"Breakfast," she says, and with a gesture invites me to sit at the table with her.

"Where did you get it?" I ask, pulling up my pants in a hurry. "Did you take my car?"

"There's a diner across the street, dummy. Didn't you notice it last night?"

"I did not. I must have been pretty out of it."

She takes a steaming egg and biscuit sandwich and sets it in front of me along with the coffee. She serves herself likewise. The coffee is black. I sip it and wince.

"I didn't know how you take it," she says, almost apologetic.

"Lots of cream and sugar," I tell her. "In case it comes up again. But thank you for getting breakfast."

She grunts as she bites into her own biscuit. I guess that means "You're welcome."

"I haven't had breakfast with anyone in years," I remark.

"Me neither, except for a john here or there," she replies. "The nicer ones." I think that counts, but I keep it to myself.

For an instant, I feel domestic. Breakfast with Jade seems like the most normal thing in the world. The feeling fades. We finish our food and coffee, gather up our stuff and abandon the room. The road calls. It's all I have, except now I have Jade too.

The road in Montana is steep, and when we climb it, the car drops into a lower gear. It doesn't sound right. The engine is complaining, but all I can do is worry about it. I can't spare the money for a mechanic to run down the problem. It's probably just my imagination anyway. When we crest a hill, I have to pump the brakes all the way down to the bottom to keep to the generous eighty miles-per-hour speed limit.

Even at eighty, the state is impossibly huge. When night comes, I stop at a rest area for a few hours' sleep without having reached the eastern border of Montana. When I wake up, it is the same as last time. Jade is in her hooker outfit, waiting for me to come out of my after-nap trip to the bathroom. Once again, she changes in the parking lot, but I'm not shy this time. As she puts her bra on, a car parks a few spaces from my own. The family of four inside it gets an eye-full. For the first time, I see her look concerned. She gets into the car, but she is only half-changed.

"Go! Go!" she commands.

"Sudden attack of modesty?" I ask as I hastily back out of the space and guide the car up the entrance ramp and onto the highway.

"Kids," she says. "The kids didn't need to see that."

I am pleased to learn that modesty exists in

her in some shape or form. There was this space in my head she had occupied that is reserved for those outside the pale of the average human. She had seemed like a doctor or a cop, ensconced in a special dimension reserved for people who I had always thought of as somewhat other-worldly. Other. Not necessarily better.

She finishes wriggling into some non-hooker clothes. I wonder how many changes of clean clothes she keeps in the bag anyway. Her bag goes into the back seat after whacking me in the head. Whatever is in there, it's heavy. Whatever is in there, I don't want to know about it, but I have my suspicions.

I really hope I don't get pulled over again.

Montana has finally come to an end, but South Dakota seems equally intimidating, another tiny hoop for me to jump through to be reunited with my fortune in Charlotte. As the sun comes up, I stop at one of an endless stream of rest stops to grab a few hours of sleep. I can't afford to get a room every night, not if I want to have money to spare. This time Jade reclines the passenger seat and sleeps with me. I look at her for a few moments as she drifts off. This time her resting face is peaceful. Then sleep grabs me as well.

I awake with a start. I forgot to set my watch. It's eleven-thirty. I had only wanted to sleep until nine. I feel lucky that a state trooper hadn't knocked on my window as I slept. Jade woke up before me, of course. I check the back seat and see her giant handbag on the floor. She hasn't done that before. Is it another bond of trust? Is there a bomb in the bag? Did she simply forget? I am amazed at how much meaning I can squeeze out of such a simple thing.

I reach back behind the seat and feel around in the bag. I want to know what's so hard and heavy in there after all. Before I can find it, Jade approaches, walking down the path from the outbuilding. I snatch my hand out of the bag. Instead of going to use the bathroom, which I really need to do, I wait for her, wondering if she saw me trying to go through her stuff.

If she saw me, she doesn't say anything, which means she probably didn't see me. Self-expression doesn't seem to be an issue for her. Once she's in the car, she takes out a prescription bottle that has no label on it and rattles it lightly.

"What's that?"

"Bennies."

"What?"

"Benzedrine," she says, her voice instructive. "To keep you awake."

"Where did you get them?"

"The trucker had plenty. I traded with him."

I want to ask what she traded, but I don't want to hear the answer. I know anyway.

"I'm not really into drugs."

"Just think of it as a Vivarin."

"What if I get pulled over with pinprick eyeballs or something?"

"Do you want to get to Charlotte quickly or slowly?"

"I want to get there quickly, but what do you care if I do or don't? Aren't you the one who just wanders from truck stop to truck stop?"

"I want to see whether or not you've got this money you say you have," she says, ignoring my question.

"Okay," I say. "How do I use them?"

"Take one when you feel tired."

Ask a stupid question…

Before we go, I call the law firm yet again. They're sick of me. I can tell from the secretary's tone. Of course, Olvido isn't available. Neither is the other attorney. Have they found the signed checks and figured out how to pay my bills yet? No, not yet, but they're working on it. I tell them they'd better get it straight before I get to Charlotte and if they don't, I'm taking my business somewhere else.

The secretary doesn't seem to be impressed despite the amount of money I've ponied up as a retainer. I need them a lot more than they need me at the moment, and they know it. I wonder how they'll react when I show up in person and fit to be tied. I can't wait to have a confrontation with them. I'm itching for a fight.

It's two in the afternoon, and I start to flag. Per the prescription, I swallow one of the pills. In about twenty minutes, I feel awake and alert—and anxious. Fidgety. I can feel them closing in. I can feel them all around me. I wish I hadn't taken the pill, and if I live, I swear I'll never take another one ever again.

It takes hours for the bennie to wear off. By eight o'clock I start to grow tired again even though there is still an hour or so of sunshine.

"I need to sleep," I tell Jade.

"Take another pill," she suggests.

"No fucking way," I tell her. "It's not an experience I want to repeat."

She sighed.

"We're never going to get there," she says.

"Again: Why do you care? And don't tell me it's

about money."

"I think I want to go to Florida," she says. "Charlotte gets me a hell of a lot closer, and if there's a cash bonus at the end of the rainbow, well, I'll take it. It's better than fucking my way to Miami."

Oh my God! I'm living *Midnight Cowboy*.

I wonder if she's going to keep being a hooker when and if she makes it to Florida, but I'm too scared or too polite or too both to pose the question. I want to point out that she can be anything she wants to be, within reason, of course. I want to tell her that she doesn't have to live this way, but I don't really know if she can do anything else. Besides, she is barely more than a stranger, even if we innocently shared a bed together. Her business is none of my business.

Or is it? Damned if I know.

We stop at a Super 8. It's shabby, like a hump-and-run. This time Jade pays. I feel ignoble about it, but I'm running out of money faster than I'm running out of highway.

They must have been having a special at the motel: the sheets had been changed. This time I don't bother with modesty. I just strip down to my underwear again and get into bed. Jade undresses to her undies. Her breasts are firm. She takes a t-shirt of mine from my clean pile and puts it on. It engulfs her.

Once again, she slips into bed next to me. We don't touch, but we're so close I can feel the heat radiating off of her body.

"How old are you?" I ask her.

"Old enough."

"Seriously. I'm not going to go to jail, am I?

"I'm twenty-eight."

I would have taken her for older if it hadn't

been for her tits.

"Okay. Cool."

I nod off while I'm facing her, drifting into sleep feeling her breathing on my face. Her breath is sweet. I don't know how that's possible, but there it is.

It seems every time I go to sleep that I wake up in some other reality. In this one, I am facing Jade, and my arm is looped around her. It is the first time I've more than casually touched anyone in I don't know how long. It is also the first time I've awakened with an erection for years and years.

The covers have been pushed down, and Jade's t-shirt has been pulled up. I stare at her nearly naked ass and shiver with an urge to plunge myself into her.

I ease off and away from her and go to the toilet, hoping she doesn't wake up before I make it. After using the commode, I take a shower. My erection is persistent. I have to do something about it. It's the first time I've masturbated in a long time. My sexual urges bedded down once again, I go out in a towel into the room to get some clean clothes, hoping that Jade is still sleeping. Of course, she's awake, sitting up in bed and stretching like a leopard limbering up to kill a gazelle.

"Nice outfit," she says.

I grunt non-commitally and grab my clean clothes and go into the bathroom again. I don't emerge until I'm fully dressed.

Jade takes her turn in the bathroom and emerges in a towel wrapped around her. She lets it fall as she rummages through her giant bag, eventually finding clothes. I don't avert my eyes, but I do try not to stare too hard. She's putting on a show, but I don't know why she feels the need to do it. I have no plans to stuff money into her garter belt or whatever one does with naked hookers. She does have a nice body. Used and abused it may be, but it doesn't look it. I lean back on the bed and wait for her to finish.

When she finishes dressing, she lies down on the bed next to me.

"Ready?" she asks breathily, taunting me as if she knows the desire I just felt for her.

"Ready for what?"

She doesn't answer right away. I feel like I'm about to get propositioned. If that happens, I have no idea what I'll do, and that scares me.

"The road," she says.

"No, I'm not," I hear myself say, even though I know I have to go. The sooner I get to Charlotte, the sooner I can resume my normal existence—normal to me, anyway. I can set Jade up somewhere and give her an opportunity to move into less exploitative lines of work that are free from truckers with tire irons, crowbars, rebar, or any other similar blunt instrument.

We both stare at the TV for a few minutes, even though it isn't on. I guess the real show is taking place inside our heads.

"I guess we could stay another day," she says.

"Money," I reply.

"I'll pay for it."

"I don't like taking your money."

"Because of how I get it?"

"Exactly. I feel like I'm using you."

"Funny, that's the same way I feel about you."

I laugh. "How are you using me?"

"I'm getting a ride," she says.

"I'm sure lots of truckers would give you a ride. You don't need me for that."

"But you don't make me put out. And with you,

I don't have to worry about turning up dead."

I have no reply for that. It's true. I'm not serial killer material. Still...

"You don't know that," I say. There is darkness in me. Doesn't she sense that?

"Sure I do."

She can see right through me. I suppose that comes with her job.

"Let's get breakfast," I suggest. "See where that takes us."

"Okay," she said, "You're paying."

Another Denny's. We sit across from each other and talk. We could be any random hookup celebrating the morning after, not just a john and a jade peeking our heads up from the personal versions of hell that we inhabit.

Our things are still in the motel room. It's a funny feeling, not having everything in the car, not being ready to go right away. It's almost like we have a home. It makes me feel vulnerable.

"What's your real name?" Jade asks. "It sure the hell isn't 'John.'" I realize that she's never called me "John." She hasn't really called me anything.

"Ken. Kenneth."

"Ken Kenneth what?"

"White. Now it's your turn."

"Trixie."

"Bullshit."

"Really. Beatrice. Trixie."

"Beatrice what?"

"Snow. Trixie Snow."

"Is that a married name or a maiden name?"

"Well, I've never been married. How about you?"

"Divorced."

"Is that when you started driving around?"

"It was about three years later."

"You have kids?"

"A boy and a girl. The boy's fifteen and the girl's eleven."

"Do you ever see them?"

"No."

"Why not?"

"They don't want to see me, and I don't want them to see me like this."

"Like what?"

"You know, like I am. Whatever you want to call it."

"I wish my father had been more like you," Trixie said around a mouthful of pancake.

"Paranoid?"

"No. Not around. He was around way too much."

We're not strangers anymore. We've crossed that line.

Trixie slams her fork down on her plate, making a sound that causes the people in the booths near us turn and look. I have a pretty good idea of why she didn't want him around, but I don't dare to give it voice. I've never met someone who's been abused before, at least, not that I know of, and I have no idea what to say.

"What about your mother?" I ask.

"Oh, she was around too. But she only saw what she wanted to see." I see a tear well up in each of her eyes, making them shine.

"I'm sorry," I say, knowing that my sorrow doesn't make one damned bit of difference.

"Well, it doesn't matter now," she says. The tears that were threatening to fall from her eyes are suddenly reabsorbed. Her hard edge is fully back in place. She is angry.

I don't know what to say, so I stay silent and push my food around with my fork. I've lost my appetite for food, and I am disgusted with myself for having admired her as a sexual creature.

Trixie is a black hole. She has a gaping wound that nothing can fill.

Our somber mood turns to fear as soon as we realize that Big Red has parked my car in. He is leaning against his truck, waiting for us. His Benson Hauling trailer has been replaced by a Workman Delivery trailer. He grins. He's glad to see us in his own sadistic way. He's not holding a tire iron, so that's something. We stop walking. I have no idea what to do except go back inside and call the police, but that's not a good idea. We're on our own.

"I'll give you your money back," Trixie says to him. "Just leave us alone."

"Oh, I want more than that, sweetheart," drawls the truck driver.

"I'll give you back double," Trixie says. "Whatever you want."

"It ain't money I want," he says. "I'm gonna get you, bitch, and your pimp too."

"I'm not her pimp," I say. Why the hell did I say that? We stare at each other for a few moments.

"What are you waiting for?" I ask. If I could, I would stare at myself for having said it. I've never considered myself brave. Trixie does the staring for me. I guess she didn't see it coming either.

He begins to walk toward us. The fact that it's broad daylight doesn't seem to phase him any. I wonder if I should put my fists up and assume a boxer's stance. It seems silly, somehow, so I just stand and wait for him, which also seems silly.

The last fight I was in was in the second grade with Dan Taylor. It was a draw because a teacher pried us apart after we got our licks in. We became friends after we came back from our suspensions.

I don't think Big Red and I are going to become friends after this.

He stops halfway across the parking lot, looking at Trixie. Trixie is holding a very large knife in front of her with both hands. It looks wicked and gigantic in her small hands. The mystery of what was so heavy in her bag has been solved.

"You're gonna cut yourself, whore," Big Red says. "You don't know how to use that." He doesn't come any closer despite his taunt.

"Are you sure about that?" she says. "Come find out." She points the tip of the blade toward him. I can see in his face that he is weighing risk versus reward.

"Hey, buddy! You want to move that truck?" someone yells behind us. He steps around us and examines the tableau the three of us are presenting to the world.

"What the fuck?" the someone asks.

Big Red retreats to his truck. It takes him a while to get it in gear, but he finally drives away.

"You guys okay?" the stranger asks.

"Yeah," I tell him, my voice trembling with leftover adrenaline and fear. "I'm glad you came along." He gives us a long look before he gets into his car and drives away.

Driving away seems like a good idea. Trixie puts her sword away. We get in the car and drive in the opposite direction of Big Red's route away from Denny's.

~~~

After a few hours of driving around, we go back to the Super 8 for our stuff. The encounter with Big Red has made me tired now that the fear has worn off, and I think Trixie feels the same way. We decide to take that extra day off the road after all. We don't articulate it. We simply fall on the bed next to each other when we get back to the room and sleep the afternoon away.

Once again I wake up first, and for a few moments I am disoriented, confused by the fact that someone is sleeping next to me and the orange light of evening is slithering its way through the room's blackout curtains. After a few moments, I remember the day's events and shudder, thinking of how close I'd come to getting a beating, or worse.

Trixie is still sleeping, her breathing long and deep. She seems very much at peace. I haven't seen her at peace until now, awake or asleep. She always seems to be aware that her blind spot is behind her, and she is constantly casting about trying to see what's coming from every angle.

I get off the bed gently and turn the TV on with the volume so low I can barely hear it. I change the channel to Headline News and see what's going on in the world. It's nothing good. World peace has not been declared. Cold fusion is not yet perfected. Cancer hasn't been cured—in short, nothing has happened that would cause me to stop my endless journey.

Trixie continues to sleep. I could ditch her. She's going to get me killed. I know she has some money wadded up somewhere in that bag of hers, and I know she's perfectly capable of producing more. However, I am responsible for her, and watching her sleep the sleep of the innocent reinforces that feeling.

I turn the TV off again. It isn't helping. I wait

for my companion to wake up. For a solid minute, I am content, basking in the glow of a perfect moment—a pause loaded with possibility, something worth waiting for. It's the way I've always wanted to feel. Trixie stirs, and the moment is over.

We drive around a little and end up in a hole-in-the-wall Italian restaurant. Either the food is excellent, or our palates are starved from eating fast food and diner food. For a while, I forget she's a hooker and she seems to forget that I'm whatever it is I am, and dinner seems extremely natural and normal like old friends reconnecting. She pays for dinner with her crumpled money, and I leave the tip.

We both feel tired when we get back to the room even though we slept most of the day away. I strip down to my boxers in front of her, and I am surprised with myself that I'm not shy about it. She takes off her pants and changes into her sleeping t-shirt. She still looks delicious. I get under the covers before I embarrass myself. She turns off the light and slides in next to me.

Time passes, but sleep does not come. I lie on my back and look at the ceiling. She is curled up next to me facing the edge of the bed. I can see the curve of her hip outlined in the darkness.

When I was married, I took sleeping with my wife for granted. I did not realize how much comfort I took in it, not until I started sleeping alone. It wasn't about sex. It was something else. Perhaps it was some primal instinct, a need for a sense of mutual protection, like sheep who hear the baying of wolves in the night and huddle together.

"Are you asleep?" I whisper.

"No." She rolls over and faces me. "I can't sleep."

"Me neither."

I pull myself back and lean against the headboard. Jade/Trixie gets out of bed and starts rummaging through her bag.

"Do you mind if I have a cigarette?"

"Only if I can have one too."

"Did you quit or something?"

"About ten years ago."

"Then I'm not giving you a cigarette. I'm not an enabler."

"You're not?"

"Blow jobs are one thing. Lung cancer is something else."

"But you're willing to expose me to sidestream smoke?"

She sighs, drops her bag and gets back into bed. "You win."

"I'm kidding. Have a cigarette. Smoke up."

"Asshole." She doesn't get back out of bed to get one, though.

"Can I ask you a personal question?" I say after a moment.

"If it's what I think it is, no," she replies.

"Fair enough. But you seem to know more about me than I know about you."

"What else do you need to know?"

"Who you really are."

"I'm not really anybody."

"I don't believe that."

"You don't think a hooker can be just a regular person? Watch TV? Try on pants at The Gap?"

"There has to be a story," I insist. "If you don't want to share it, I understand."

"You don't understand. You don't understand anything. You just keep on driving."

"I'm sorry," I say. "You're right. I won't ask again." I can feel her slowly decompress next to me, limbs gone rigid soft and pliant once more.

"I like you," she says. "You're easy." She leans her head on my shoulder. It's still there the next morning.

Before we hit the road, we find a laundromat. We dump all of our clothes together in one of those giant washing machines, including her work uniforms. When they're dry mine go into my clean basket and hers are folded and stuffed into her big bag. I offer to put the bag in the trunk, but I know she won't part with it. It is all she has in the world. Trust can only go so far.

There is always the road. I used to dream about gray roads and flashing white lines every night when I first started driving, but I don't anymore. The road has become so integral a part of my being that it is infused into every cell of my body. Movement has become my state of rest.

We've made some progress, but not enough. Our extra day had a price tag, and I wasn't ready for the bill. We've navigated our way south now, skirting the borders of Nebraska, Iowa, Kansas, and Missouri. Unfortunately, there won't be any more motel pit stops along the way. It's probably better this way. Being alone in a room with Trixie will eventually lead to heartache.

I pull off into a rest stop outside of Kansas City after twelve hours on the road. Like before, I set my watch to wake me in three hours. This time, though,

Trixie sleeps next to me in the car. She doesn't wander off to turn tricks. I feel a certain triumph because of that, but I'm not sure why.

When we awake, we use the bathroom and buy sodas and snacks from the vending machines, paid for by the loose change I keep in the ashtray of the Ford 500. I drive for another four hours until I'm wracked with the need for sleep again. I'm reaching a point of diminishing returns. Three hours of sleep here and there reclined in the front seat of my car are no substitute for the full seven-and-a-half hours of sleep I need to function. I'm in a rough place. I need my money for gas, but if I fall asleep at the tiller, it will all be for nothing. I may not want to live a normal life, but I don't want to die either.

A tiny voice inside me tells me that things would be better if Trixie would ply her trade, and I am disgusted with myself. The idea is up there with the notion of selling my daughter into slavery for some paltry sum of money that will stave off starvation today only to starve again tomorrow.

I take the nearest exit and pull the car into the parking lot of a Burger King.

"Lunch?" Trixie asks.

"Money count," I reply. I proceed to count my money, including all the change and random dollar bills in the car. Two hundred forty-seven dollars and nineteen cents. That's it. That's all. What have I been thinking about, spending an extra day in a hotel room, much less a hotel room to begin with?

I do some mental calculation. I can fill the car with gas six times before the dough runs out, and that makes no allowance for food or motels. Estimating roughly four hundred miles per tank, it will take a minimum of three tanks to get to Charlotte.

Meanwhile, Trixie has been counting her money.

"Six hundred and twelve dollars," she says.

It is a veritable fortune.

"Is it enough?" she asks.

"We don't need it," I say. "I've got enough gas money to get us to Charlotte, as long as we're careful. No more hotel stays, though. We just barely have enough for food."

"Let me help."

"You've helped enough," I say. "And I shouldn't even have let you help that much."

"Why not?"

"It's your money. You earned it."

"Didn't you earn yours?"

"No. I inherited it."

"You mean you're rich?"

"I wouldn't say 'rich.'"

"You don't work, and you have money. All you do is drive around the country. Sounds like you're rich to me."

"Only if I can get my business sorted out in Charlotte. Right now I'm poorer than you."

"Then fucking deal with it. I'm not going to sleep in a car when I can sleep in a bed," she says. "If you want to stay in your car, that's fine. You can sleep in the fucking parking lot if you want to." She turns away from me and looks out the window.

"Okay," I say. "But all this is a loan. When we get to Charlotte, I'm going to pay you back, every penny."

"You're going to do better than that, I hope. There better be Skittles at the end of this rainbow."

I do not know if Trixie is a reward or a penance. She's starting to look like an uncut birthday cake, and I'm starting to want a slice. Desire. Desire is an enemy. Any Buddhist monk could tell you that. In the past five years, I have wanted for nothing, nor has there been anything I wished to acquire. All of my needs were met. My money made me ascetic. Pure.

Until now.

Now I am full of desire. I want to get to Charlotte. I want to get the money I need to return to life on the road. It's odd that my money can quell my desires, but that is the nature of my universe.

There is something stirring in me, and I'm having a hard time tapping it down. I do not know if it is lust or optimism or the false domesticity of life on the road with Trixie, but I have to stop it. I need to lose myself in the drive once again. It's the only way to be safe.

We stop for the night in Louisville, Kentucky, or some place close enough as to make no difference. Trixie pays. Once we stash our stuff in our room, we walk across the road to a truck stop for something to eat because we're thoroughly worn out from the drive, and we can't stand the thought of sitting in the car for another minute. The buffet isn't bad, and we belly-up to it more than once.

When we cross the street back to the motel, it doesn't take more than a swift glance to realize that something is very wrong. All the windows of my car are smashed. The hood is bent from having been pried open.

We both realize what's happening at the same time, but we don't have an opportunity to do anything about it. A breath of air tickles the back of my neck. I turn...

~~~

...I am laying on the pavement of the parking lot. Trixie is making a noise somewhere between a scream and a sob. The back of my head hurts so badly that the pain astonishes me. I sit up and put my hand to the back of my head. It comes away bloody. Trixie's face is also bloody. The blood streams freely from her nose. Her eyes are already starting to blacken. I don't imagine I look any better.

A small crowd has gathered. They do nothing to help. They simply stand and gawk. I slide over to Trixie on my behind and wrap my arms around her until she stops screaming. It takes a minute or two.

I try to ask Trixie if she is okay, but the power of speech eludes me. I take a look around. Beside my car, I see my wallet. I know without checking that it has been emptied. Trixie's bag has been upended and her things scattered across the lot. I know that she has been robbed as well.

Police lights flash against the side of the motel. The little crowd disperses except for a few who part to let the policemen by. The tall one shines his flashlight on us and immediately calls for an ambulance.

"No," I manage to croak.

"What?" says the cop.

"No money," I whisper. I have health insurance, but if the premiums haven't been paid, it's just another worthless card.

"Don't worry about that now. Tell us what happened."

I tell them about the car and waking up on the pavement. Then they turn on Trixie, and she tells them how I was knocked out, she was beaten, and then we were robbed. We both know who it was and why, but naturally we don't tell the cops that. It wouldn't make any difference anyway. He's long gone, cloaked in anonymity and the night and the high cab of a big rig. He'll never be found. It's just as well. I'd try to kill him if I got the chance and probably get myself killed in the process.

The ambulance arrives, followed by another. One set of paramedics starts on me and the other on Trixie. They ask me a bunch of questions. I stammer out answers as best I can. I want to know how Trixie is doing, but they won't tell me. I want something to relieve the pain in my head, but they ignore me. They hoist me onto a gurney and strap me in and load me into the ambulance. I try to sit up and find Trixie, but the belts hold me fast.

The motion of the vehicle is very soothing, and I want to go to sleep, but the paramedics keep waking me up.

Suddenly I am far from the pain in the twilight of consciousness that lies between dreaming and wakefulness. The ambulance stops. I am unloaded and wheeled into an emergency room bay. A man with a tire iron watches me, but when I try to focus on him, he fades away. I'm told to keep still for an X-ray. Blood is drawn. A plastic tube is run into my arm.

I ask about Trixie. They tell me she's okay. I ask to see her, but I am ignored again. A mosaic of hieroglyphics begins to cloud my vision, and I cease...

...my eyes snap open. The room I'm in smells like a hospital. I try to look around, but I can't move my head. The pain leaps onto me, and I am in agony. A man with a tire iron stands at the foot of my bed. I scream and scream for help until someone comes. Suddenly the pain recedes, and I am...

~~~

Jason Feingold

As I awake I am no longer in agony, but the pain is still there—distant, like a second echo, but there nonetheless. A woman whose face is a mass of swollen and bruised flesh sits in a chair next to my bed. I realize that the woman is Trixie.

"You're awake," she says. "It's about time."

"How long?" I hiss.

"Three days."

"Are you okay?" I ask.

"Nothing broken. Still hurts like a bitch, though."

"Me?"

"He fractured your skull. Your brain was bruised."

Trixie reaches out to the rail of my bed and presses the call button for the nurse. He comes quickly. Not a good sign.

"How do you feel?" he asks, his accent thick from some foreign land.

"Been better."

"What's your name?"

I tell him.

"Who is the president?"

I tell him that, too.

"What year is it?"

I have no idea, and I inform him as such. He clucks at me.

"Two out of three isn't bad," he says. "Do you know where you are?"

"Hospital."

"Where?"

"Kentucky, I think."

"Good."

"When can I leave?" I ask.

"That's up to the doctor," the nurse tells me. "I

doubt it's going to be today. Maybe tomorrow. With that, he wanders off.

"Karma's a bitch," I say to Trixie.

"I'm so sorry," she says. "I'm sorry I got you into this."

"I'm a big boy. I knew it could happen."

Actually, the thought never crossed my mind. I figured the confrontation in front of Denny's would be the last we saw of him. I thought anything else was just some paranoid delusion.   "What are we going to do?" Trixie asks. Her voice is thick. It must hurt her to talk with her mouth so swollen.

"I'm going to call my goddamn idiot lawyers in Charlotte and get them to wire us some money. "Hand me the phone." She hands me the cheap hospital phone. I dial the number of the lawyer's office, but the phone won't let me call long distance. I slam the phone down on the bed tray, and the equal and opposite reaction rocks through my skull like a spike.

"Stay still," she commands.

"We have to get out of here. We need to go to the motel and get our stuff from them before they throw it out."

"Too late," she informs me. "By the time I got back there our stuff was long gone. It was a long walk. All we've got was what was in my bag, minus the money, and your empty wallet. I don't think I'm going to be able to make more money looking like this."

"I wouldn't let you even if you didn't," I tell her. I am not a pimp. "Your hooking days are over. I'm going to take care of you."

"Don't tell me what I can and can't do."

"I am going to take care of you," I repeat, "but you're right. It's not my place to tell you what you can and can't do. I'm sorry." She nods at me. Apology accepted.

"How have you been surviving while I was out?"

"I've been sleeping here and eating your meals. The nurses are looking the other way. They feel sorry for me."

"Where's my car? My cell phone was in it. And there's some money in the ashtray."

"I don't know. They towed it somewhere. I'm sure the money is long gone."

"Does it run?"

"No. It's totaled. The asshole wrecked the engine."

"Maybe we can sell it for parts."

The situation is worse than my worst case scenario. I've thought about what might happen with no car and no money, but I hadn't accounted for being injured too. We are well and truly fucked.

My stay in the hospital lasts a week. Trixie stays with me. We share my delightful hospital food. Eventually, I am allowed to sit up, to stand, and finally to walk by day five. I don't have to piss in a bottle anymore. The nurses scrounge up scrubs for Trixie and take her laundry home with them to wash it for her. We are grateful to them to the point of tears.

We are adept liars, Trixie and me. As more people ask us our story, it evolves into this: We are a married couple. I lost my job in Seattle, and we decided to go home to our native North Carolina. We're down on our luck. We were robbed of all the money we had.

The hospital raises a few hundred dollars for us before I am discharged, and we are out on the street, her in clean clothes carrying her giant bag, me in used clothes, two hundred and forty-two dollars between us. We sit on a bench in front of the main entrance of the hospital. Before we begin to formulate a plan, I take a fistful of quarters to call the lawyers in Charlotte. I resent every coin I pump into the pay phone.

The lawyers still have no idea what they're supposed to be doing for me, nor will they condescend to wire me any money. I threaten to sue them, but neither begging nor blustering gets me any cash.

"We need to get to Charlotte," I say, returning to the bench that has become our temporary home. "Maybe we can take the bus."

Another telephone call nixes that possibility. Two fares cost more than what we've got; and besides, we have to eat. We've both lost weight sharing hospital meals. We decide to go find something to eat. Maybe things will look better on a full stomach.

We walk along the town's main drag and find a greasy-looking diner. A "Help Wanted" sign decorates the window front. The diner is very crowded, and it looks like only one waitress is working the entire place.

"We need jobs," I say to her when she finally makes her way to our table. I just blurt it out without thinking about it. Trixie gives me a funny look.

"How come I've never seen you around here before?" she asks.

I give her the condensed version of recent events. Trixie's faded bruises actually make themselves useful as a testimony to our story.

"You poor things. Well, I have jobs," she says. "I need a dishwasher and a waitress. Got any experience?"

"I've washed dishes before," I assure her.

"I've waited tables before," Trixie says. I have no idea if she's lying or telling the truth.

"Can you start right now?" she asks.

I stand up. "Where's the sink?" I ask.

I've been washing dishes for three hours. My arms, shoulders, and back are killing me. I give myself a break and peek into the dining room. I see Trixie carrying three plates balanced on her arm with a water pitcher in the other hand. She has done this before. I wonder how she transitioned between waiting tables and prostitution. I guess she gets tips either way. It's another mystery to contemplate when I resume my endless journey.

I wouldn't be in this colossal fuck-up if it weren't for Trixie, but I wouldn't be able to get out of it without her.

Money used to make me free. Now it is the tyrant that enslaves us.

It is the end of the shift. Trixie and I are walking to a hotel. We each ate a free meal. We're tired. Trixie's tips are enough to stay for the night, but not for anything else.

I try to be upbeat, but I realize that we're just running in place. We're surviving, but we're not getting any closer to Charlotte and my money. Getting jobs and a free meal was a *deus ex machina*. I doubt we've got another one coming.

We climb into bed, exhausted. I'm almost asleep when the realization hits me:

"We're married," I say.

"What?" Trixie says.

"We represented ourselves as husband and

wife. It's a common law marriage. We're married."

"But we were lying," she says.

"I'm not sure it matters," I say.

"Is there common law divorce?" she asks.

"We've only been married a week," I joke. "We're still on our honeymoon. It's too soon to be talking about divorce. Don't you want to give us a chance?"

"I already gave marriage a chance. It didn't work out." She's serious.

"You told me you were never married."

"I lied. I didn't want to talk about it."

"I'm sorry your marriage didn't work out."

"I'm not. He was a bastard."

I already know where this is going.

"He beat you."

"Yes."

"So you left and divorced him."

"He left."

"So you're divorced?"

"No."

"I don't understand."

"I killed him." She spits the words out fast like she has a mouthful of black bile. I don't know what to say. I have no words. I can feel her tense up next to me. I put my hand on her shoulder in an attempt to show her that it's okay, but she shrugs it off.

"When Rick and I were dating, and when we got engaged, he was kind, gentle and sober. A week after we were married he suddenly drunk, mean, and rough.

"The first time he hit me was on our honeymoon. We were in Niagara Falls. He wanted to go to Madame Tussaud's Wax Museum, and I wanted to go to the Ripley's Believe It or Not Museum. We fussed at each other a bit. Rick settled it by punching me in the stomach."

"Are you fucking serious?" I finally ask.

"Yes."

"It was downhill from there. I got beatings for overcooking pork chops or spilling wine on the carpet."

"Why didn't you leave?"

"He loved me. I loved him. It sounds stupid now, but that was what it was like. I just had to get things right to make him happy. That's how I felt.

"One day I went to the mall and spent too much money on clothes. At least, that's how Rick saw it. That beating earned me a cracked rib. At the hospital, I told them I'd fallen down the stairs. I don't think they believed me, but they didn't say anything.

"The beatings stopped for a while after that. I think the trip to the hospital scared him. A couple of weeks later I forgot to pack his lunch. He broke my arm."

Her hand finds mine. We hold hands as the story unfolds. Her grip is tight. She continues. Her voice is flat and getting flatter as she talks.

"I told the hospital that I had broken my arm falling down the steps again. I didn't think they'd remember, but they did. After they set my arm and put my cast on, a woman came into my emergency bay and told Rick to go wait in the lobby. He did what he was told, but he gave me a look that said he would kill me if I talked.

"Her name was Alice. She grilled me for an hour until I admitted that Rick was beating me. I begged her not to tell anyone because I really believed Rick would kill me, but she called the police anyway. They took me to the magistrate's office, and I swore out a warrant and a restraining order. They put Rick in jail.

"The cops brought me home. They told me if Rick showed up or called that I shouldn't talk to him or let him in. They said I should just call 911."

"I'm guessing that you didn't," I say.

"You guess correctly," Trixie says. "When he came back he was all contrite. He gave me a houseplant. He told me he loved me and said he'd never hit me again. Jail had made him think, he said."

"And you believed him?"

"I loved him," she says simply.

"But..?"

"No buts. I really loved him. And for a month things were great. He was calm, sober, thoughtful and nice. He brought me flowers. He told me he loved me. It was great."

Trixie pauses here. I know what's coming next. I wait to see if she will tell me anyway.

"One night he came home drunk," she says matter-of-factly. "He started hitting me. He didn't even give me a reason. After he was done punching and kicking me, he dragged me to the bedroom and tried to rape me."

"Is that when you killed him?"

"No. He passed out before he could finish raping me."

"Why didn't you call the cops?"

"Because they wouldn't have done anything. I'm the idiot who let him back into the house."

"I'm sure they would have..."

"Don't be so sure. You don't know what it's like. Men stick together."

She lets out half a sob, then bites it off like a chunk of beef jerky.

"I went to the kitchen and grabbed the biggest knife I had. Then I went to the bedroom and stuck it through his neck."

Tears are streaming from her eyes, but she looks angry. I can see the hard lines of her face glisten in the darkness.

"There was so much blood. He tried to take the knife out of his neck, but he only cut his hands. He got real still. I'd never seen anything as still as his dead body."

Trixie is silent, sniffling in punctuation of the silence.

"I couldn't go to the cops because I'd killed him after he attacked me, not during. I had no way to get rid of the body. I had two options: jail or the road. So I hit the road.

"That's when you became a..." I can't finish the sentence.

"Uh huh. I needed a job where they don't ask for social security numbers and positive ID. I found jobs where they paid under the table, but they didn't last. If I had found this diner sooner, it might have been a different story. Instead, I ran out of money, and I needed to keep moving, like you. Just for different reasons. And it's better than taking a beating."

Trixie had gone from an abusing father to an abusive husband. It seems like a trite and hackneyed tale until you're in the presence of someone who's lived it. It is a Technicolor ghost, visible and intangible at the same time, haunting her, but she's unable to grasp it and cast it out.

I am suddenly furious. I get out of bed and punch a wall. It hurts my hand like hell.

"Why are you so mad? Are you going to turn me in?" she asks, a slight panic rising in her voice.

"No. Rick had it coming."

"Then why'd you punch the wall?"

"Because your husband isn't here for me to kick the shit out of."

She begins to cry, the sobs she had bolted down springing up all at once. I want to tell her not to, but I know it's a stupid thing to say. I force down my anger and get back into bed and hold her until she stops. She slobbers all over my t-shirt, so when she stops, I take it off and wipe her face with it. She puts her head on my shoulder, and we fall asleep.

I have never crossed a line that can't be uncrossed. Even when I set out on my journey, I always had the option to stop. When I abandoned my children, I still had the opportunity to go back, to go from absent to present, from motion to stillness. The woman beside me doesn't have that option. She's crossed a bridge and burned it behind her, but that doesn't mean she isn't being chased. Her demons are real. Mine are only inside me. Fleeing was our only choice.

It's early when I wake up. I ease Trixie's head from my shoulder to a pillow and rise and stretch. I feel rested—energetic, even. I peek out from behind the blackout curtain. The sun is strong on the horizon. Another day. Another hope to be realized or quashed.

"How do you know I won't kill you too?" Trixie asks from behind me. I jump. I didn't hear her coming toward me.

"Are you?"

"No."

"That's how I know."

"I could be lying," she says.

"But you're not."

"How do you know? I could be a black widow or something. I've done it before."

"If you were going to kill me, you'd have done

it when I had cash and a car. They're no point in killing me now. You'd lose those valuable dishwasher dollars." I swallow. "Besides, I'd never hurt you."

I turn around and look into her eyes. They're brown. I hadn't noticed that before. I want to kiss her, and I nearly do, but I know it's not the right thing to do or the right time to do it, so I step away from the window and flick on a lamp.

"I need to get some clothes," I say. "Maybe there's a second-hand shop around here somewhere. I need to see about my car."

"Okay," she says. I do not know if she is disappointed or thankful that the kissing moment has come and gone unconsummated. I'm not sure how I feel about it either.

Our shift at the diner starts at 11:00, so we have time to get some of those things accomplished. While Trixie is in the shower, I call the police and find out where my car is. We'll have to take a cab. It's six miles away. We don't have time to walk. Besides, I need to save up my energy to wash the endless piles of dishes.

I pay the motel clerk for another night and ask him to call a cab. He takes us to the garage. I'm pretty sure he took us the long way, but I don't know enough about the layout of the town we're in to object. However, we make it there in due time. My car is sitting off to the side, a tarp draped over it to hide the ugliness of what was done to it.

"Your car is basically totaled," the mechanic tells me. "You should make a claim on your insurance."

"I don't have insurance," I admit. I'm sure it's been canceled along with my credit cards for non-payment.

"In that case, unless you've got a lot of money you don't need, it would cost way more to fix than its worth. What do you want me to do with it?"

"I'd like to junk it," I tell him. "Would you be willing to buy it from me? For parts?"

He thinks about it.

"Two hundred," he says.

"Five hundred," I counter.

"Two hundred," he repeats. "I'll never get five hundred from a junkyard." I'm pretty sure he's lying. It's a fairly new car.

"Can you make it three hundred?" I ask. "I'm really hard up."

"Two-fifty."

I look at Trixie. She gives me the slightest of shrugs.

"Okay."

He doles out twelve twenty dollar bills and a ten and is nice enough to let us call a cab.

"Oh. I've got your GPS navigator and tracker," the mechanic says before the cab arrives. He hands me the electronic devices. I recognize my navigator, but not the little black box.

"You've made a mistake," I tell him, looking at the thing. "I don't have a tracker or anything."

"No mistake," the mechanic says.

Trixie and I exchange looks.

I take my GPS back.

"Throw the tracker out," I tell the mechanic. "I don't need it anymore."

"Mind if I keep it?"

I shrug. "Be my guest."

When the cab arrives, I ask the driver to take us to a thrift store close to the diner.

"He must have put it on the car at that Denny's," Trixie says.

"Why didn't he take it back when he was done

beating the shit out of us?" I ask.

"He must have forgot."

This driver doesn't give us the grand tour, and the fare is half as much as it was to get to the garage in the first place.

At the store, I buy four shirts, two pairs of pants, a belt, and five pairs of underwear. The underwear isn't used, thank God. Trixie buys two outfits for herself along with a pair of practical shoes. Our wealth is now measured in the number of garments we have and the number of nights we can stay in a cheap motel. The only way we're ever going to make it to Charlotte is if we hitchhike there. I realize with a lump in my throat that it may come to hitchhiking.

When we get to the diner, the owner has a uniform ready for Trixie and whites for me. It's a relief that we don't have to mess up our street clothes. It'll save us time and money at the laundromat.

"About your pay," she says as she hands us the clothes.

I see visions of W-4's dancing in my head. I'm okay, but Trixie can't fill one out. She might as well walk into a police station and confess.

"I'd rather keep Uncle Sam out of it," she says. "You can keep all your tips, honey," she says to Trixie. "You I'll pay six an hour, cash."

"Works for us," I say.

"Great. Get changed and get to work."

There's a lovely stack of dishes waiting for me at the pot sink, and no matter how fast I wash them the pile never shrinks. I ache all over. I've never done manual labor, even before I got my inheritance. All of the dirty dishes speak of a diner that does a good trade. We've hitched our busted-down wagon to a greasy star.

When I peek out at Trixie, she's working a special kind of sexy in the dining room. I don't know if I'm jealous or not. However, I can see that the front pocket of the apron of her uniform is both weighed down and bloated from cash and coin. I wonder if she was a waitress before she headed out on her own endless run.

Maybe we'll get out of this yet, I think.

We work until closing, ten hours later. I have to wait until the end of the week to get my money, but Trixie has enough cash and coin to sustain us, and we're eating for free. Even so, we're tired and still recovering from the beating we took, and the walk to the motel we're shacking up in seems just a little further than it did yesterday.

Somewhere along the way, Trixie's hand slips into mine. I pretend that it's no big deal, but of course, it's a big deal. It's different than any other time. This is a show of affection. It thrills me to think that she may be thinking about me in the same way that I'm trying not to think of her, trying and failing.

We're still holding hands when we open the door to our motel room. I close it behind me, and then we stare at each other for an eternity of seconds. Then Trixie shakes her head. Our hands unlatch.

We watch TV for an hour or so in our pajamas—underwear and t-shirts—while sitting up in one of the beds. We begin to fall asleep, so I use the remote to kill the TV and reach over to turn off the light. Instead of falling right to sleep we both squirm around until we are holding each other. I can feel her breasts rise and fall against my chest. I don't doubt for an instant that she can feel my erection against her leg, but she doesn't move away. I stroke her back with my free right hand while she plays with my hair with her left.

"You need a haircut," she says.

"I know. I don't like haircuts."

"Why not?"

"I don't like to be touched."

"What do you call this?"

"That's different," I say, and it is.

In a few moments, she is asleep. I think about sneaking out of bed and going to the bathroom to relieve myself in the shower, but I stay where I am. It takes a long, long time for sleep to find me.

We work the early shift at the diner. Breakfast. Breakfast doesn't cost much, and therefore customers don't tip as much. My job actually gets harder. Getting solidified egg yolk off of a plate takes an almost superhuman effort. I discover to my surprise that the work doesn't hurt my body as much. I'm getting used to it, and dishpan hands to boot.

When I take a break and peek into the dining room, Trixie is getting a lot of "honey's" and "darling's" and "sweetheart's" tossed in her direction. A lot of the men stare at her ass as she walks by or her tits as she walks toward them. I know it shouldn't bother me, but it does. One jackass actually reaches out to goose her, but she deftly slips away from him. I start to leave the kitchen to confront him, but Trixie sees me coming and shakes her head no. She can handle herself.

I have no claim on her. I have no right to be angry on her behalf, and I have no right to be jealous of her. Yet I am all of these things. She is mine to care for. She is mine to protect because I let her into my car. So I return to my pot sink and continue washing my endless stream of dishes and pots and pans.

I lose myself in the work like I used to lose myself in the endless drive. It is only when Trixie lays her hand on my shoulder that I realize it is time for our break and our free meal. We eat in the dining room in the lull between the breakfast and lunch crowd.

"How do you do it?" I ask as I dig into my Denver omelet. "How do you put up with all that shit from the customers?"

"You get used to it," she says, picking at her muffin.

"You shouldn't have to," I continue.

"It is what it is," she says. I've always hated that phrase.

"Well, we won't have to do this too much longer," I say. "We should have enough to get to Charlotte in a couple of weeks if we're careful." Trixie looks up at me and then down at her muffin again. She pushes her plate a few inches away from her.

"What, you want to stay?" I ask.

"It's not so bad," she says. "It's not a luxury cruise, but we have enough to get by. Isn't that enough? I could stop running. You could stop driving."

I shake my head no.

"We can do better. We can get you new papers. A whole new identity. I can set you up wherever you want to go and give you a head start. You could go to college, or..."

"What makes you think I haven't been to college?"

"Well, I just assumed."

"I was in my third year when I dropped out to marry Rick," she informs me, huffy and bent out of shape.

"I'm sorry. I shouldn't have assumed."

There is silence between us.

"What did you major in?" I ask. I don't want the silence to take root.

She murmurs something.

"What?"

"Hospitality," she says.

I try to keep a straight face, but I can't. In a few seconds, I go from giggling to raucous laughter. Trixie shoots laser beams at me out of her eyes, but I see a grin escaping her lips. Suddenly she is laughing as loud as I am. The few people in the dining room look at us strangely. It's not often that life presents you with such a clear and present case of irony. But as with all comedy, there is an undercurrent of pain.

Suddenly, the days have turned into a week. It is easy to lose track of time, living as we do, day to day, hour to hour. I think about my inaccessible fortune less and less. We work, we do laundry, we sleep in on our day off or when we work the late shift. We have some money saved up, but I don't know how much it is. I give mine to Trixie for safe keeping when I get paid. It can't be much, though. We're still paying for our motel room by the night, and we're still pumping quarters into washing machines, and we're still eating out when we get hungry, and it's not our shift at the diner.

We sleep together every night, sometimes simply next to each other, sometimes in the embrace of the other. I make it a habit to shower at night, so I can jerk off, but it's barely enough to keep me from making a sexual overture toward Trixie. There is always that line we can never cross. It outlines our existence; it circumscribes every interaction. It would only take one prick to pop the balloon in which we live, and we'll never find another.

Another few days pass by. I realize that Trixie and I have barely been apart since I let her into my car less than two weeks ago. I've joked that we are married, but I never spent this much time with my ex-wife, except perhaps during our honeymoon. She had her work, and I had mine. We would be together for a few hours after the evening chores were done before bedtime. And there were weekends, of course. And the children. Once the children came, there was hardly any time at all.

All that is in the past. Now there is only Trixie and me and our tiny workaday world.

We have a reserve of two hundred dollars at any one time. With the motel, the laundry, and meals, we are barely keeping pace. There isn't enough for us to go to Charlotte by bus, but I don't think Trixie would be able to pay for the room on tips alone. If I went to Charlotte by bus, she'd have no reserve money to draw on and quite possibly end up in the street. I'm afraid she'll go back to hooking, and that I cannot countenance. I no longer have anything against hookers, but since I've learned what dangers they face my sole desire is to shelter Trixie from it. So I say nothing about it.

"We should get an apartment," Trixie says out of nowhere during our meal break.

"What?" I ask. I heard her, but I need a moment to compose myself.

"It's got to be cheaper than paying for a motel every night," Trixie says. She's right. It would be.

"There'd be utility bills," I say, advocating for the devil.

"It'd still be less," she insists.

"Okay," I acquiesce. "One bedroom or two?"

"An efficiency."

"We'll be bumping elbows in one of those."

"It's cheaper."

She has a point.

After Trixie goes back to waiting tables, I strike up a conversation with Beverly, the owner of the diner. I ask about furnished apartments.

"Are you two planning on staying?" she asks.

"Sure," I say. It is, of course, a lie. I'm a multi-millionaire doing dishes in a hole-in-the-wall diner in Kentucky, but, of course, she doesn't know that. I wonder what she would do if she found out.

She narrows her eyes at me.

"For how long?"

"Hard to say," I say evasively. "Months, at least."

"Okay," she says. She writes a name and number on the back of a restaurant check pad. "Call this guy. Tell him I told you to call."

"I appreciate it." It's amazing how grateful I've become for the little things.

The apartment is laid out shotgun-style—a living room, a kitchen, and a bedroom in the back. It's ugly as hell, and it needs a coat of paint after plastering the cracks. It's three hundred a month, semi-furnished, and in walking distance of the diner and the local Walmart. For an extra fifty a month we can also rent a washer and dryer. We spring for them. We're thoroughly sick of the laundromat.

We check out of the motel at last and carry our few possessions easily to our new digs. I've never been happier to have my own place. I'm even happier than the first time I got my own place when I was in college.

I plop down on the battered sofa. It's surprisingly comfortable. I hope it isn't infested with fleas. Trixie sits right next to me. I put my arm around her shoulders like I'm trying to steal second base.

"Home crap home," I say, surveying our little empire.

"I've had worse," she says. "Imagine a place where the cockroaches don't run when you flick on the lights."

"No, thank you."

The apartment has no bed. We can either buy one or sleep on opposite ends of the couch. We opt for a mattress. We hoof it back to the thrift store and buy a full-size mattress and a set of sheets. We arrange to have the mattress delivered for an extra twenty bucks. We then walk to Walmart and get a hermetic plastic bag for the mattress, since neither of us wants to die of a used mattress disease. I almost tell her that I once owned a large piece of Walmart, but I doubt she'd believe me. We pick up a few sundries and walk... home.

But this town is not my home. I don't speak the language. I can barely understand it. I don't know my way around. I can't get around; at least, not very well. No car. I don't even know where the movie theater is. Yet here I am, digging in. In a week, I already have more crap than will fit in the trunk of a car. I've planted my flag.

Suddenly, I'm scared.

They can find me. I showed my ID to get this apartment. They're already on their way.

My paranoia hits me all at once. What the hell have I been thinking? I can't stay still. I have to get on the move. But there is no way to get on the move, no medium of transportation except hitchhiking, which I'll never do. Between us, we haven't got enough money to buy a bicycle, much less a car or a ticket to

Charlotte. In fact, we're lucky to have landed on our feet in the first place. We're lucky to be running in place.

Trixie puts her stuff in the top three drawers of the dresser. She hangs her few blouses in the closet where somebody thoughtfully left a few wire hangers. I sit on the floor with my laundry basket in front of me. I don't know what to do. If I don't put them away, Trixie will wonder why. If I do, I could lose all my clothes if I have to run. In the end, I pack my things in the Walmart bags and stuff them in the drawers. It is as close to the best of two worlds that I can come. The world of stillness. The world of motion.

No TV, no radio, no internet, and no telephone. We are cut off from the world in our shotgun shack kingdom. There is nothing we need to know, nobody we need to call, and nobody to call us. We only have each other for diversion.

Trixie lays her head on my lap and reads a romance novel she bought at the thrift store. I should have picked up something to read, but the idea of reading to pass the time seems new to me. For five years, I've been moving, and all my time has been divided between driving, resting from driving, and the most basic grooming and maintenance activities.

I brush an errant lock of Trixie's hair behind her ear. She smiles but does not glance up from her book. She feels safe. I can tell from how relaxed her body is. I can tell because her jaw is not clenched shut. I can tell from her exposed throat. She is safe with me. I am pleased with myself that this semi-feral woman has been resocialized by me.

Or is it the other way around?

~~~

It's Friday. I pocket the cash that Beverly pays me. Between us, we have $400 or so, and the rent and utilities don't need to be paid for another three weeks. There is enough for us to get to Charlotte and to my lawyers' office to straighten out my financials, and some to spare.

"We can leave," I say to Trixie as we walk back to the apartment.

"You can leave," she says. "I can't."

"Why not?"

"I don't have photo ID," she says.

"You need photo ID to take the bus?" I am incredulous.

"Bus, plane, train, you name it," she says.

"I had no idea."

"Of course you didn't. Why would you?"

"I can go by myself," I tell her. "Once my mess gets straightened out I'll buy a car and come back for you."

"To give me my reward?"

"To give you anything you want."

She laughs in my face. It angers me.

"You won't come back," she says. "Your kind never do."

"What the hell is 'my kind?'"

"People who live on the radar," she says. "Above board people."

"Are you kidding? I've been moving for five years. Running," I say in self-defense.

"What are you running from?"

I don't know the answer to that, so I remain silent.

"You're running from yourself," she says.

"You're running, too."

"That's different, and you know it. My demons

are real. They have bright shiny badges and handcuffs, and the best I'll get is life in prison."

"How can I prove to you I won't desert you?"

"You can't because you will."

"That's not fair, and you know it."

We climb the rickety steps that lead to our apartment. I open the door and usher her inside before entering myself. I look at our beat-up couch and ancient washer and dryer and the mattress on the floor in the room where we sleep. It looks like a flophouse, or at least what I imagine a flophouse looks like.

"Trixie, we can do so much better than this," I say softly because I'm still angry.

"No, we can't. You don't understand. You don't understand anything. You're just 'A. John.'"

I should never have said that. It stings when it's hurled back at me. I turn back to the door and let myself out without a word.

"Bastard!" she shouts after me.

I have no place to go, and I have no money to spend even if I had a place to go. All the cash is in Trixie's bag. Still, I walk around for a few hours to ease my anger and wonder why Trixie's going off the deep end now that the finish line is in sight.

Perhaps she thinks I'll squirm out of the deal I made to pay her back and more. I'm sure it wouldn't be the first time someone's broken a deal with her. Being a wanted woman severely limits her in so many ways. I could help with that. What good is all my money if it can't buy me what I want? I can extend my shield of money around her. I'm sure I could set her up with a new identity, social security number, passport, and everything else. I can free her.

Does she even want to be free? Has she ever

been free?

She's gone from college to marriage to taking it on the lam. Being on the lam is the freest she's ever been, perhaps, but her life is still curtailed by the constant threat of getting caught. Perhaps she can't imagine living without it. I don't know, and I certainly can't pretend to understand, not with her.

I walk back to the apartment. I don't know what I'll do or say when I get there, but I know it's the place I need to be. I quicken my pace, but I'm too late. When I open the apartment door, I find two hundred dollars piled on the floor with the words "Good Luck" scrawled on a torn-out flyleaf of her paperback. She is gone.

For the first time in weeks, I sleep alone.

When I get to the diner for my next shift, I apologize to Beverly for Trixie clearing out, which is the least I can do since it was she who she pulled our fat out of the fire after we were beaten and robbed. Instead of heading to the finish line in Charlotte, I stay and wash dishes. My two hundred forty a week provides me with enough for rent and utilities and food, but not much else. It's fine. I don't need much else. I'm just another undocumented worker slaving away at a job with no future and no past except for the backlog of dirty pots and pans and dishes that greet me with every shift.

I have become the hermit I wanted to be. The shotgun shack is my cave. I walk to where I need to be. I buy enough basic food to sustain me. I buy a radio and tune it to some talk radio station and keep the volume low, so it sounds like there are people in the next room. It is enough to keep me sane, or at least sane-ish.

~~~

At the supermarket, I accidentally swipe one of my credit cards out of habit instead of reaching for my cash. I expect it to be declined, and I prepare to be embarrassed. It is approved instead. I ask for change and call the law firm on the first pay phone I can find. My new lawyer, Ms. Oglethorpe, tells me that she's glad I called. Everything has been paid up and made current, and the law firm paid all the late fees incurred by the lack of payments. I have money again—millions if I want. I can do anything, which seems the same as not being able to do anything.

When I get back to the shack, I lay all of my credit cards out on the floor that also serves me as a table and a shelf. I have three Visas from three different banks, two MasterCards, an American Express Platinum and even a Diner's Club card which I've rarely used, but I have it nonetheless. I meticulously bend all the cards until they break into quarters, except one. I need one. More than one is paranoid. Overkill. Ridiculous.

I go to the diner and give Beverly my notice. I wish I could give her two weeks, but I don't have the time, and time is a factor. I'll send her a small fortune later in return for all she did for us, but I don't tell her that because she'd never believe me.

After quitting my job, I go to the nearest car dealer and buy a used Mazda something-or-other for nine thousand. I don't need a luxury car, just one that has an air conditioner and won't fall apart anytime soon.

While the dealer is doing the paperwork, I borrow a computer and compile a list of truck stops and rest stops that follow the most direct route to Florida, where she once told me she wanted to go. On a blank sheet, I sketch Trixie from memory. I wish I had a picture, but she would never have let me take one, even if I had a camera. Fortunately, the sketch isn't bad. I hope it will be enough.

I'm on the road again. I don't take anything from the apartment except my clothes. I leave the key on the kitchen counter and say goodbye to the place with a tinge of regret. There are good memories here, and part of me wishes I didn't have to go. But I must.

Now I'm on the road again, just like the man said.

In a movie, I'd find Trixie in two cinematic minutes flat. I'd drive for a while, and she would pop up over the horizon with her thumb out, waiting for me to rescue her. That's too easy, though. There's nothing easy about Trixie, not even when she's Jade. She's going to make it hard on me, and I'm going to want to give up the search a hundred times. But I won't. I'll never quit. I'll hire detectives if I have to. My pockets are deep. I can afford to up-end all the stones and peer into all the dark corners of the world.

I owe Trixie. I miss Trixie. I may even love Trixie. It's all scrambled up in my head. All I really know is that I have to find her. For the second time in a matter of weeks I have a destination—it's nebulous, but a destination nonetheless, and when I find her... Well, what can I say? I don't know what will happen, but I do know that we've learned to speak the same language.

The road is different now. Before it enfolded me and kept me safe in its infinitely long arms. Now it is a fickle friend; it takes where it used to give. It has become my enemy. It swallowed up Trixie, and it took her away. It interposes itself between her and me. As I drive forward, it pushes back at me with a concrete hand, slowing me down at every turn.

I am still frightened as a drive along the

highway, but this is a different kind of fear. I'm afraid I won't find her despite all my resources. I'm afraid she'll disappear like I did five years ago. Of course, when I disappeared, no one cared enough to find me.

I thought Trixie had put down roots wherever we were near Louisville, but whatever roots she grew there were too fragile, and the soil too loose. They tore away the minute the breeze stiffened into a wind.

I force myself to be as bold as I ever have, but, still, the first truck stop is the hardest. I walk around the place showing truckers my sketch and asking if they've seen a girl named Jade. More than one trucker asks me suspiciously if I'm a cop. I cook up a story about Jade being my sister and me trying to find her. I embellish it with details as I repeat it over and over again. Most are sympathetic. Some don't give a shit. A few are openly hostile. I wonder when I encounter the hostile ones if they're the one who put the crease in the back of my skull or, even worse, if they'll put one in hers.

I catch word of her at a truck stop somewhere in Georgia.

"Yeah, I seen her back near Athens," the trucker tells me. "There was a bust. She got rounded up just like all them other whores."

"Know where they took them?"

"To jail'd be my guess." Ask a stupid question...

"Do you know where it is?"

"Can't help you there, bud."

I thank him. I plot my route to Athens. I have no fucking idea what I'm going to do when I get there.

The police station in Athens strikes me as the first logical place to start. Actually, it's the only thing that occurs to me. It makes me feel like I'm in the belly of the beast. I'm nervous. Scared, even. I'm about to lie through my teeth to the cops, and if I get caught the chances of being charged with aiding and abetting a fugitive are virtually guaranteed. Or maybe I could lie or lawyer my way out of it. I don't know.

I'd envisioned a gruff sergeant sitting behind a high counter to be my first point of contact with the police. Instead, there's a middle-aged woman in civilian clothes working at a desk behind a window with a hole in it.

I take a deep breath.

"I'm looking for my sister. She's missing," I tell the receptionist. "I think she might have been arrested here."

Now I can add making a false report to the police to my list of felonies.

"Have a seat. I'll call a supervisor."

I sit and fidget. At first, I try to calm myself, but then I realize that my trembling voice can work for me. I am the nervous, grief-stricken brother on a mission of last resort.

After an interminable amount of time, a woman dressed in a pants suit with a badge and a gun on her waist comes out into the lobby/waiting area.

"Can I help you, Mr...?"

"White. Ken White."

"I'm Detective Sergeant Samantha Bryant. Let's talk in my office." I follow her to a cubicle, and we sit down. She takes out a legal pad and starts writing. Damn.

"I think my sister may be in jail here," I tell the detective.

"And why is that?"

I try my best to look sad and ashamed.

"Prostitution."

"What's her name?"

How could I not be prepared for this most basic question? I can't use her name. If I give her real name and they don't know it, they're going to find out she's presumably wanted for murder.

"Well, that's a complicated question. Her real name is Rebecca White, but she doesn't go by it."

The detective turns to her desktop computer and presumably types in the fake name I gave her. If there is a real Rebecca White in their system, I'm screwed.

"She's not in the system. What name does she go by?"

"I'm pretty sure her street name is 'Jade.'"

Detective Bryant turns back to her computer.

"We have a Jade Doe in the system. She's locked up in the county jail. But you say her name is Rebecca White?"

I nod nervously.

"Middle name?"

Fuck.

"Look," I say to the detective, "Do you have children?"

"I'm not here to talk about me," she replies coldly.

"My sister. She's sick. She's on drugs, and she's got, you know, mental problems. I'm want to take her home to North Carolina and get her help. She has a chance to have a normal life, but an arrest record is going to make it that much harder."

"She's never been arrested before?" the detective asks.

"No. Not that I know of, anyway."

"What exactly do you want me to do?"

"All I want to do is take her home and get her well. Please."

"How do I know you're not her pimp?"

I try to sound insulted. "Do I look like a pimp?"

She says nothing, but she's thinking so hard I can smell the wood burning.

"Do you have some ID?" she asks. I take out my North Carolina driver's license and show it to her.

"All right," she relents. "I have to call the ADA and get the charges dropped. In the meantime, you can wait in the lobby."

"I can't tell you how much this means to me," I gush. "Thank you so much!"

"If you want to thank me, get her the hell out of Athens and don't come back."

"You'll never see us again," promised. I don't think I've ever been more sincere about anything in my life.

I'm in the lobby, sitting in a chair, waiting to find out if my bullshit worked. It takes two hours. Two hours of staring. Two hours of watching people come and go. Two hours of watching officers go back and forth.

I want to run. I've got that hollow feeling in the pit of my stomach that we all get when we're in love or in really deep shit—or both.

Detective Sergeant Bryant emerges from the recesses of the station.

"You're all set. You can pick her up at the jail." She tells me how to get there.

"Thank you."

"Remember what I told you."

"Yes, ma'am."

I'm halfway there when I realize the flaw in my plan. There's no way that Trixie knows what alias I picked for her. When they call her, how will she know to respond? I have to get them to call for "Jade," or I'm screwed. Once again I have the urge to run away, but I calm myself. I have to do this, no matter what. I have to.

The jail has a lobby, and a man behind a sheet of glass much like the police station does. There are a few tired benches lining the walls, and the place has an odor to it that I've never experienced before. It is less than pleasant, like a high school gym with a peeled onion sitting in the middle of it.

I stroll up to the window, trying to give the appearance that I am both self-assured and completely above board. It occurs to me that a lot of people probably do the same thing, both inside and outside. Well, there's no reason I should stand out.

"I'm here to pick up Rebecca White," I tell the jailer behind the glass. "I don't know if she'll respond to it. She's got...problems. She goes by the street name 'Jade,' though." Everything rests on the name they use to call her.

"It'll take a few minutes to get her discharged," the man says. "You can have a seat." He points to the worn benches against the wall of the lobby. They feel as uncomfortable as they look. I guess there's no need to coddle prisoners or their families.

My nervousness is like the Richter scale. With each passing minute, I am ten times as nervous as the minute before. I sit there for forty-five minutes, sweating bullets. I occasionally fan myself with my hands pretending I am hot, even though I'm not. It's just for show, and I have no idea if I'm a good actor or not.

Trixie finally emerges through the locked door

that divides freedom from incarceration. She's dressed in her hooker outfit, and there's a manilla envelope sticking out of that giant bag of hers.

"Becky!" I shout. I run across the room and embrace her. She is less than enthusiastic, which feeds the story I've fed the police even more palatably. Then I push her back by the shoulders and say, "Do you know how worried Mom has been?"

"I'm sorry, Ken," she says. She bursts into tears—real tears. "I'm so sorry. I just want to go."

"Let's get out of here." I start maneuvering her towards the door. "You need to call Mom and Dad." We quickly let ourselves out of the front door.

"Gold Mazda," I whisper. We both head for the car, get in, and we're gone, hopefully heading out of town. We're silent for awhile like we were in the beginning.

"How did you find me?" she asks after a while.

I take the sketch of her out of my pocket and toss it onto her lap.

"I went to every truck stop and rest stop between Louisville and here, showing that picture to every driver who'd talk to me. Then I found out about the sting the cops ran and took a chance you were here. It worked."

"How did you get me out?"

"I sweet-talked one of the detectives. It doesn't matter. Just tell me you didn't use your real name."

"I'm not stupid," she says. "I only told them 'Jade.'"

"Then we should be free and clear. But I want to get out of Georgia as soon as possible, just in case."

"Where'd you get the car?"

"I bought it with a MasterCard. When we get to South Carolina, I'm going to trade it in and get another one."

"Why?"

"It's my first prison break. I don't want to get caught."

She was silent for a few moments.

"Your money," she says. "Your money came through."

"Finally, yes. But you never believed I was telling the truth, did you?"

She ignores the question.

"It's a nice sketch," she says. "Did you draw it?"

"Yes."

She softens for just a second. "I don't think anyone's ever done that for me before."

"It's not like I had a lot of choice. I didn't have a picture of you."

"No, you didn't."

Several silent moments pass. There are a lot of trucks on the road, and they make a lot of noise when I pass them. I'm used to the soundproofing of more expensive cars.

"Why did you leave me?" I finally ask.

"Because you were going to leave me," she says. "You were never going to come back, so I did the leaving first. I didn't want to stay in that horrible apartment alone, so I hit the road."

"But you left bus fare."

"Just in case."

"I would never have abandoned you. You should have known that."

She wipes away an angry tear.

"Did you..?" I can't bring myself to say it.

"Go back to my old life? What do you think?"

"I think I'm disappointed."

"I told you before. I'm not the hooker with the

heart of gold. I'm just a lot lizard. That's all."

"I know what you were. I know what you told me. I believed you then, but I don't believe you now. You may not have a heart of gold, but you've got a good heart under all that armor. That's what I believe."

"Then you're stupid."

I let that sink in.

"Yeah, maybe I am stupid. But that doesn't mean I'm wrong."

Once we're over the South Carolina line, I stop at the first car dealership I can find. Trixie is still in her hooker outfit and doesn't seem inclined to change, but I proceed with the transaction despite the frank stares. I trade the Mazda for a Lincoln MKZ. The bastards only give me five grand on the trade even though I paid nine thousand when I bought it a few weeks ago. I suppose I should haggle, but I don't have the time or energy for it. No matter. All of the irregularities are overlooked when I pay for the car outright with the MasterCard.

It takes about an hour of waiting while they detail the car and do the paperwork, so Trixie and I end up sitting around in the customer lounge ignoring each other. She is a magnet for intrusive eyes, and I am a magnet because I'm sitting next to her. I return every stare until the strangers drop their gazes to the floor. Eventually, Trixie seems to become conscious of what's going on around her and goes into the bathroom and changes into her jeans and flannel shirt.

Not only is the Mazda gone, but the temporary tag that could be used to find me again is gone as well. In South Carolina, as it turns out, they don't issue a t-tag; instead, they use a license-plate-sized dealership logo as a temporary. The police won't be able to run a license number while we're moving, in the remote chance that they're looking for us. It is another layer of protection between us and the world, thanks to money and coincidence.

In four hours we are back on the road again. Unfortunately, the gap between us is even wider in the larger car.

"Where are we going?" Trixie finally asks.

"Home."

The word pops out of my mouth as suddenly as the idea enters my head. For the first time in my life, I know where it is. I know how to get there. Its seed is inside me, and it has been all along. All I have to do is plant that seed, and home will grow up all around me. It doesn't matter where. Trixie taught me that in Kentucky. We were at home there, at least for a little while. It doesn't matter where I plant my fig tree. Home will blossom in the desert or on the beach or in a forest somewhere. I can take it with me wherever I go.

"So where is this home of yours?" she asks.

"Charlotte. At least for now. I have a house there. You'll like it."

I can try to reconnect with my children. Perhaps I can earn their forgiveness for my absence, for all the years we lost. I'll buy Trixie a new identity, just as I promised, and we can live together. We can look at each other with new eyes. We can feel what it's like to be at rest again.

"Besides, Charlotte is where I'll get you your Skittles," I tell her.

"What?"

"You said that you expected Skittles at the end of this rainbow. Fairy tales do come true."

"I don't need your money. I'm just fine on my own."

"No, you're not. Don't let some sense of misguided pride screw up your future, because right now you haven't got one. What happens in a year? Five years? Ten years? What happens if you get caught? Have you thought about that?"

"What happens when you get tired of me?" she asks. "Have you thought about *that*?"

"That's never going to happen." It is as close as I've come to telling her I love her.

Her face softens for a single beat of a hummingbird's heart.

"I'll be just fine. Let me out." She's trying to be gruff, but I think it's a lie, so I call her on it. I jerk the wheel and pull over onto the shoulder of the road. I slam the car into park and reach over her to push the passenger door open.

"Fine. Get out. If all this doesn't mean anything to you, then fuck you. You're welcome for getting you out of jail. Goodbye." I turn my head toward the driver door's window so she can't see my face. I am close to tears. These are the hardest words I've ever spoken. Can't she hear the tremble in my voice? I do not want her to go.

She reaches into the back seat for her big bag, her tiny allotment of things in a universe full of material objects. She puts one leg out the door and hesitates. For an endless moment, she has one foot in my world and one foot in hers. She can't straddle them both forever. Eventually, she'll have to make a choice.

I can wait. Either way, I'm going home.

After a teaching career, Jason began writing, with works published in journals, anthologies, and collections. When not writing, he reads, keeps house, is a husband, raises a son, chases dogs, and occasionally ventures out into the world to buy groceries.

Thank you to the Wapshott Press sponsors, supporters, and Friends of the Wapshott Press.

Muna Deriane
Kit Ramage
Rachel Livingston
Laurel Sutton
Thomas Loper
Kathleen Warner
Ann and John Brantingham
David Meischen
John O'Kane
Suzanne Siegel
Toni Rodriguez
LindaAnn LoSchiavo
James and Rebecca White
Robert Earle and Mary Azoy
Steve Misuraca
Alice Frances Wickham
James Wilson
Phil Temples
Richard Whittaker
Ann Siemens
Kathy Bonagofsky

The Wapshott Press is a 501(c)(3) not-for-profit press publishing work by emerging and established authors and artists. We publish books that should be published. We are very grateful to the people who believe in our plans and goals, as well as our hopes and dreams. Our website is at www.WapshottPress.org. Donations gratefully accepted at www.Donate.WapshottPress.org.

www.ingramcontent.com/pod-product-compliance
Lightning Source LLC
Chambersburg PA
CBHW070508130626
46555CB00003B/1205